PRAISE FOR THE SERIES

The Shark Rider

"This is a great follow-up to Prager's first Sea Guardians novel, sure to hook more fans."
—*Booklist*

"Tristan, with his talent for conversing with sharks, and his marine biologist creator, author Ellen Prager, use this fascinating plot to explore ecological avenues, proving that even kids can have an awesome skill that can save the planet."
—*Foreword Reviews*

". . . amazingly imaginative, tautly written, just-slightly-magical, fancifully fun series. Warning: You're likely to learn a lot too."
—Carl Safina, ocean scientist and conservation expert and author of *Beyond Words* and *Nina Delmar*

"Earn your sea legs and go on an exciting eco-adventure . . . It's fun, funny, informative, and my favorite part is where the characters must outrun a hurricane. And where do they get their information to track the storm—The Weather Channel, of course!"
—Stephanie Abrams, on-camera meteorologist for The Weather Channel

The Shark Whisperer

"Like author Rick Riordan, who mixes adventure with Greek myths, [Prager] writes books that include action and humor, science and sea creatures."
—*The Washington Post*, KidsPost

"... an underwater Harry Potter, sure to inspire readers to want to dive in and experience the ocean for themselves."

—Sylvia A. Earle, National Geographic
Explorer-in-Residence and founder of Mission Blue

"Those who know Prager well wouldn't be astounded to find her delving into the realm of ocean science and youth fiction. Throughout her career, Prager always made it a priority to involve young minds."

—*The Miami Herald*

"A wonderful read that grips you from the very beginning. This empowering story of a group of young people who band together to save the oceans and change the world is a terrific adventure."

—Philippe Cousteau, explorer and environmental advocate

"Appealing characters, non-stop adventure, and a sprinkling of humor blend with . . . education about marine life and the ocean in fun and interesting ways."

—*VOYA* Magazine

"Ellen Prager takes her readers on an exciting, action-packed adventure into the mysterious world of the deep, with an edge of fantasy that only the most vivid imagination could conjure up. A rollicking ride of fun, that also imparts to her young readers a valuable education about the marine world, and the fascinating creatures that live in and around it."

—Sam Champion, anchor at The Weather Channel,
former weather anchor for ABC News

"Here's one book that as a father and an ocean lover I can wholeheartedly recommend. Take the adventure, dive in, and happy reading!"

—Bob Woodruff, ABC News correspondent

STINGRAY CITY

STINGRAY CITY

TRISTAN HUNT AND THE SEA GUARDIANS

BY
ELLEN PRAGER

WITH ILLUSTRATIONS BY
ANTONIO JAVIER CAPARO

mighty media JUNIOR READERS

MINNEAPOLIS, MINNESOTA

Published by Mighty Media Press Junior Readers, an imprint of Mighty
Media Press, a division of Mighty Media, Inc.

Illustrations: Antonio Javier Caparo
Design by Mighty Media, Inc., Minneapolis, Minnesota
Interior: Chris Long · Cover: Emily O'Malley
Editor: Lauren Kukla

Library of Congress Cataloging-in-Publication Data
Names: Prager, Ellen J. | Caparo, Antonio Javier, illustrator.
Title: Stingray City / by Ellen Prager ; with Illustrations by Antonio Javier
Caparo.
Description: First edition. | Minneapolis, Minnesota : Mighty Media Junior
Readers, 2016. | Series: Tristan Hunt and the Sea Guardians ; book 3 |
Summary: "Thirteen-year-old Tristan Hunt has enough to worry about
with girl troubles, his parents, and trying to keep his extraordinary underwater abilities a secret. But when Tristan and his similarly gifted friends
are called upon to investigate the disappearance of stingrays and other
ocean life in the waters off Grand Cayman, the stakes are higher than
they've ever been before"—Provided by publisher.
Identifiers: LCCN 2015044223 | ISBN 9781938063701 (paperback)
Subjects: | CYAC: Camps—Fiction. | Ability—Fiction. | Stingrays—Fiction.
| Marine animals—Fiction. | Wildlife conservation—Fiction. | Cayman
Islands—Fiction. | BISAC: JUVENILE FICTION / Action & Adventure /
General. | JUVENILE FICTION / Animals / Marine Life. | JUVENILE FIC-
TION / Nature & the Natural World / Environment. | JUVENILE FICTION
/ Fantasy & Magic.
Classification: LCC PZ7.P88642 St 2016 | DDC [Fic]—dc23
LC record available at http://lccn.loc.gov/2015044223

Manufactured in the United States of America
Distributed by Publishers Group West

For all my fans and supporters who continue to provide encouragement, inspiration, and fun!

TABLE OF CONTENTS

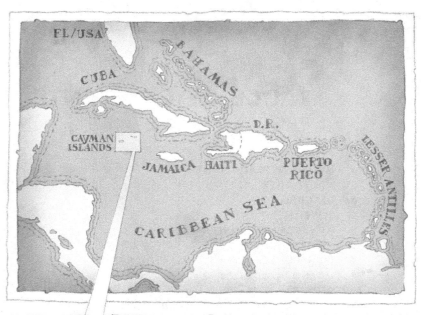

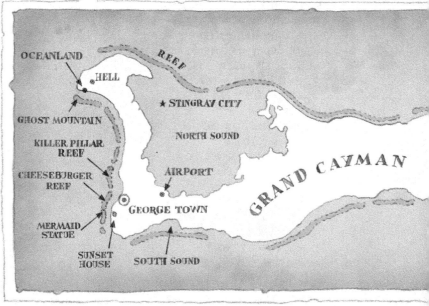

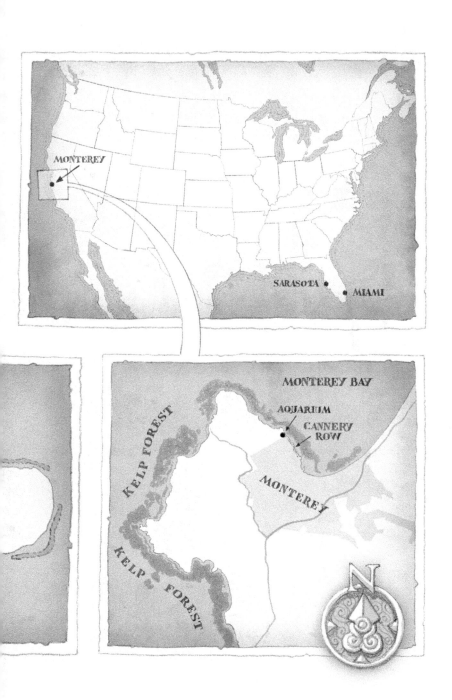

1

HIDING IN PLAIN SIGHT

THE FIVE YOUNG TEENS STOOD HORRIFIED, STAR-ing at the creatures on exhibit. Trailing behind the animals' glowing orangey-gold bells were white, ruffled feeding arms and tentacles seven feet long! The tentacles reminded Tristan of giant strands of dark-red spaghetti. With one big difference—mega-long pasta wouldn't sting the bejesus out of you.

"No way!" Tristan announced. "I'm not going in there."

"Like, dude, me either," Ryder agreed.

"Not a chance," Hugh added.

"Come on, you guys," Sam chastised. "One of us has to go in and do it."

"If you think so, then you go in," Rosina snarled.

Sam shook her head. "Are you nuts? I'm not going in there."

If you could ignore their potential to pack a terribly painful sting, the sea nettles in the display were actually quite beautiful. Lit up and drifting against a brilliant blue background, the jellyfish looked like slow-motion dancers costumed in long, crimson streamers and pale ruffles. At the center of the tank, however, things were not so pretty. Ongoing collisions had created a jumbled, twisted mess—a massive floating tangle of stinging jellyfish. And it was growing larger by the minute.

It was nighttime at the Monterey Bay Aquarium, and the teens from Sea Camp were on untangling duty. Since arriving at the aquarium, Tristan Hunt and his friends had been regular volunteers during the day and on special assignment after dark. But this was an assignment absolutely no one wanted.

Tristan flicked back the strands of brown hair that constantly fell over his face. He leaned his tall, gangly body closer to the tank, staring at the snarl of sea nettles. His best friends and camp mates, Sam Marten and Hugh Haverford, stood beside him. They each wore jeans and a light-blue polo shirt with the aquarium logo on it. Hugh's slightly pudgy face looked even paler than usual, especially against his short and neatly combed dark hair. Sam fidgeted nervously, twisting her long, sun-flecked, wheat-colored ponytail with her fingers. Tristan's other camp mates, Rosina Gonzales and Ryder Jones, had stepped back as if the lengthy tentacles could somehow wiggle their way through the thick acrylic viewing window.

The aquarium's senior jellyfish curator was with the teens. He stood nearby, watching. "So, who's going in?"

No one volunteered.

"Figured that would be the case," the man said. "You'll be pretty covered up, so the stinging won't be *too* bad. No one's ever died from it or anything."

Tristan couldn't tell if he was joking.

The jellyfish curator held out a hand curled around five straws. "Whoever draws the short one is the lucky—or should I say *unlucky*—detangler."

Sam closed her gray-blue eyes and chose first—a long straw. Ryder went next. As he stepped forward, his wild, blond surfer hair trembled ever so slightly. He came away smiling, holding a similarly lengthy straw. Hugh then nervously grabbed a straw—long. That left Rosina and Tristan. Rosina remained where she was, so Tristan stepped up. Silently praying, he chose. Relief washed over Tristan as he stared at the long straw in his hand.

Rosina promptly turned the moldy-green color of cottage cheese gone bad. Shaking her mop of perpetually disheveled brown hair, she muttered, "I . . . I can't go in there."

The man took Rosina's arm. "This way, young lady. We'll get you suited right up."

The others watched as the young teen was led, shell-shocked and mumbling, to the door that led behind the jellies' exhibit.

"Hugh, I thought you could speak jelly," Sam whispered. "Maybe you could help. You know, just direct them to untie themselves or something."

Hugh shook his head. "No, thanks. I may have done some pretty crazy things earlier this summer, like riding that shark. But I was under duress, probably in shock, and that was crazy—this is just plain stupid."

Tristan nodded, very glad he wasn't the one going into the tank. He had enough problems just untying his shoelaces or doing anything that took even a small amount of dexterity. On land, he was still pretty much a klutz.

The teens could see Rosina and the curator moving around behind the twenty-foot-long exhibit. Tristan decided to check out some of the other jellyfish in the gallery while they waited for her to get ready.

Famous for figuring out how to keep jellyfish alive and on display, Monterey Bay Aquarium had one of the best collections of both common and exotic species. The first tank Tristan came to was a five-foot-high, transparent cylinder filled with flying saucer-shaped pink moon jellies. Each was about a foot across. He'd seen this species in the Bahamas and Florida. Supposedly, their sting was pretty weak. Tristan preferred not to be the fact-checker on that one. Next to the moon jelly display was another cylindrical tank. This one held dozens of small, white-spotted jellyfish. They were yellowy-brown, mini-cupcake-sized, polka-dotted creatures with clusters of short, frilly feeding arms. Next to the tank, a small speaker blared fast-paced disco music. Tristan leaned closer to the tank. He could swear the white-spotted jellies moved in short, rapid bursts, perfectly in beat with the music.

He moved to the next tank. It contained small, plum-colored blubber jellies pulsing to a different tune. Their bells resembled dark-purple, sideways-bouncing, blubbery rubber balls trailing clusters of weird, triangular-shaped arms. Tristan then moved to a darkened corner of the exhibit, where perhaps the strangest of the bunch were on display—jellyfish that lay on the bottom of the tank with bioluminescent pearls of light atop their flattened bells. After staring at the seemingly starlit creatures for a few minutes, Tristan hurried back. He definitely didn't want to miss any of the action at the big sea-nettle tank. On the way, he passed displays with upside-down, egg-yolk, and lion's mane jellyfish.

"Here she goes," Sam announced.

Tristan made it just in time to see Rosina climb up a ladder to the top of the sea nettle tank. A wetsuit top and hood covered all but her hands and face. The hood gave her chipmunk cheeks and emphasized her big, fearful eyes. The jellyfish curator stood beside the ladder and urged her on. Rosina paused, looking around. Tristan figured she was probably searching for the nearest exit. Rosina then took a there's-no-way-out-of-this deep breath and tentatively stuck a hand into the sea nettle tank. She reached cautiously toward the huge, drifting knot of jellyfish. One of the free-floating jellies bumped her hand. Rosina drew back so fast, Tristan thought she would fall off the ladder.

It was then that Tristan noticed the strands of transparent goo flowing from Rosina's fingers. "Nice slime," he said, referring to the mucus that regularly oozed from Rosina's hands when she was in seawater. When it came to their special ocean talents, she was the only one in the group who had developed mucus deployment skills.

Rosina slowly reached back into the tank and gently touched the jelly's bell, pushing it out of the way. Her hand trembled as she then nudged the jelly's tentacles and feeding arms away from the massive tangle. The look on her face was not what Tristan expected—puke-inspiring pain. Instead, Rosina appeared pleasantly surprised.

Rosina reached more confidently into the tank and undid a twist of tentacles and feeding arms. She then leaned over and submerged her entire head and upper body. Using both hands, she began to swiftly untangle the sea nettles. Rosina came up for a breath and then leaned back in. Soon the massive snarl was undone, and all the jellies were once again drifting freely about the tank.

The other teens stood stunned in front of the exhibit. Deep in thought, Hugh pondered the scene. "It must be the mucus."

"What must be the mucus?" Sam asked.

"It's like how clownfish coat themselves in mucus so they don't get stung by the anemones they live in."

"Oh, I get it," Tristan said. "It's her slime. It's protecting her from the stinging."

Sam smiled. "Sweet!"

"Like, she can have it," Ryder said.

Rosina popped up from the water grinning. She

reached back into the tank and stroked one of the jellyfish like it was a cuddly pet. She looked up and waved with a slow-motion, I'm-the-queen wave. Tristan swore she was looking and smiling specifically at him. It was a bit disturbing. Rosina was usually not the most pleasant of people, and she rarely smiled. But then again, ever since he'd saved her from drowning in the boulder pool and helped her escape from the psycho spa in the British Virgin Islands, she'd been acting strangely nice to him.

A little while later, Rosina rejoined the group. Hugh and Sam high-fived her. Ryder gave her a cool head nod. Rosina then stepped toward Tristan as if she was about to hug him. He shuffled backward awkwardly, nearly tripped, and held out a fist. Rosina fist-bumped Tristan, all the while staring kind of dopily at him. Sam rolled her eyes and Hugh grinned knowingly.

The jellyfish curator joined the group and gave Rosina a hearty pat on the back. "Well done, young lady. That was quite impressive."

The trip to Monterey and its world-famous aquarium had come as a complete surprise to Tristan and his friends. Just over a week ago, they'd been at Sea Camp in the Florida Keys, waiting alongside the other campers for a ride home. They were leaving several weeks earlier than normal. All of the teens were disappointed; some were ready to revolt. They loved their summers spent training at Sea Camp. At the age of twelve, each had been invited to the camp housed at the Florida Keys Sea Park. The teens all had rare, but very cool, genetic abnormalities. Their bodies contained traces of the ancient genes that have allowed animals to adapt to life in the sea. This gave the teens some truly unusual and amazing abilities in the ocean. At Sea Camp, they learned how to use their special talents and trained for missions to help the ocean and marine life.

Thirteen-year-olds Tristan, Sam, Hugh, Rosina, and Ryder were second-year campers, or Snappers. For them, the early end of camp that summer was doubly crappy. Like the other teens, camp was the best part of their year. They didn't want to leave early. Even worse, they were the ones being blamed for the early departure. Earlier that summer, they'd helped to expose creepy wackjob Hugo Marsh as the person responsible for a series of fish kills in the British Virgin Islands. Unfortunately, along the way, the teens had also revealed their secret ocean talents to Marsh and one of his partners—the shark-killing, kidnapping billionaire J.P. Rickerton. Tristan and his camp mates had run into that evil nutcase before. With the campers' help, Marsh had been captured and taken into custody, but Rickerton had escaped. Sea Camp's director, Mike Davis, said Rickerton was on the run. But just to be safe, the camp was temporarily shut down and the teens sent home early—except for the Snappers. Rickerton knew about them and what they looked like, so the camp leaders decided it would be best if the Snappers went somewhere to hide for a little while . . . just to be safe.

Monterey Bay Aquarium was a perfect hiding place. During the summer, the place was swarming with visitors and teen volunteers. Tristan and the other young campers would blend right in. They could hide in plain sight.

By day, the teens were regular volunteers helping to direct people to different exhibits and working at the aquarium's touch tanks. As volunteers, the teens told people how to handle the sea creatures properly and explained their biology. The big pink sea stars were everyone's favorites. Tristan and the others happily explained how the sea stars walked on hundreds of suction-cupped tube feet, that they could survive out of the ocean for hours by pumping themselves full of seawater, and about their amazing powers of regeneration. If a sea star lost an arm, it could grow another one. Of course, the teens didn't tell onlookers about their own special healing capabilities in the ocean. Once regular visitor hours were over, the campers were assigned somewhat more unusual tasks.

Rosina's detangling duty was the teens' last job of the night. On their way out of the aquarium, they passed the enormous Open Sea tank. Swimming within the more than one million gallons of water were hammerhead sharks, sandbar sharks, a school of fast and beefy tuna, and a few extremely large stingrays. Also in the tank was a small bat ray. Tristan stopped and waved to the bat ray. It was about a foot and a half across, black on top, white underneath, with a short whip for a tail and a large, bat-like head.

"Hey, isn't that the ray you got moved from the touch tank?" Hugh asked.

Tristan smiled. "Yeah, looks pretty happy now that there's no touching going on." He thought back to the campers' first night at the aquarium. He'd been asked to find out what was wrong with a small ray in one of the touch tanks. Most of the skates, small bamboo sharks, and bat rays in the shallow outdoor pool swam happily around, letting people feel their soft, velvety skin. But one bat ray stayed in a corner and refused to go anywhere near human hands. To get it to talk, Tristan had to climb into the pool and sit next to the reclusive bat ray. At first, the ray simply ignored Tristan. But when it realized he wasn't going away, the creature finally opened up for a heart-to-heart, bat ray-to-teen talk. The creature spilled its guts, luckily not literally. It proceeded to explain in agonizing detail why it didn't like being touched by humans: germs. The bat ray was a serious germophobe. Tristan had tried to convince it that human hands didn't carry any germs that would harm the ray (as far as he knew). But no matter what he said, the bat ray was convinced human hands were laced with germs that would make it deathly ill. Tristan eventually concluded that the ray was totally neurotic, bordering on having OCD, and would never make a good touch-tank occupant. He convinced the aquarist in charge to move the bat ray into the big non-touching Open Sea exhibit.

As Tristan watched the bat ray swim alongside one of the big stingrays, a hammerhead shark swam across the tank right next to the viewing window. Then it did a U-turn and swam back.

"What's it doing?" Sam asked.

"That's the shark with the weak left eye that kept swimming in circles. Remember, the other night when you guys were with Hugh at the giant octopus tank, I was here helping the hammerhead learn how to swim straight. It's just showing off now."

"Speaking of the giant octopus," Hugh said. "I better go by the tank and check things out."

The teens took a short detour to the giant Pacific octopus exhibit.

"Looks okay to me, dude," Ryder noted.

Hugh pointed to a large pink sea star at the base of the rocks in the display. "Yeah, except I think that's one of the sea stars from the touch tank."

The teens looked closer at the five-armed crawler. Suddenly, a large red arm with giant white suckers slithered to the sea star and lovingly caressed it.

"Oh boy, that guy's a real monster, all right," Rosina snickered.

"What can I say, he's a friendly giant octopus," Hugh said.

"Yeah, and still a kleptomaniac," Tristan laughed.

The octopus was infamous for its after-hours thieving. At night, when all the visitors and staff had gone home, the huge red octopus liked to slither out of its tank and take things. In the morning, the staff often found play toys from the otters' tank stuffed into and under the rocks in the octopus's tank. Several signs had been jimmied off the walls and had also ended up in the exhibit. The octopus seemed particularly fond of signs that read *Stop Here* and *No Flash Please*. One morning, the staff even found a Barbie doll in the giant octopus exhibit. A young visitor must have left it behind in the aquarium. It gave everyone a real start when they found the doll, upside down, legs sticking up with its head stuffed into the mouth of a giant anemone, in the exhibit. Sometimes the octopus would kidnap other creatures, like the sea star, and place them in its tank as well.

"C'mon, he's trying to break the habit," Hugh said. "It took me three nights of convincing and, of course, the video footage from the security cameras, to get him to confess. After that, the guy in charge agreed to put some toys in his tank at night and add a few new tank mates."

Tristan had been with Hugh for moral support on one of the nights he was trying to get the octopus to confess. Hugh was used to working with Old "six arm" Jack, the elderly octopus back at the Rehab Center at camp. But Monterey's bright-red octopus was about ten times larger—hence the name *giant* Pacific octopus. Its four-foot-long arms were lined with huge white suction cups, and its bulbous head was nearly two feet across. Hugh had become pretty good about swimming with sea creatures and talking to them, but the giant octopus kind of freaked him out.

As they walked out the aquarium exit, Hugh said, "Remind me to tell someone about the kidnapped sea star."

The group was staying with Pete, the aquarium's director of communications, at his house nearby. As Tristan got ready for bed, he wondered what new tasks they'd be assigned next at the aquarium. For the most part, he liked their nights there. He felt like they were accomplishing something useful and helping out in ways other people couldn't. Plus, at night it was quiet with only a few people around. The daytime crowds made Tristan nervous. He was constantly looking over his shoulder, wondering if people were staring at him or the others weirdly or if Rickerton had discovered where they were and had sent a goon or two to spy on them. Back at camp, Tristan had hoped they'd be able to help search for Rickerton. But once Director Davis sent the teens to the aquarium to hide, suggesting that they may not be safe at home, Tristan lost a little of his nerve.

2

NIGHT DUTY

The next night, the teens were assigned two new tasks: one in the sea otter enclosure, the other in the giant kelp exhibit. They decided to go to the kelp exhibit first. It was one of the aquarium's centerpieces, meant to showcase the lush beds of giant kelp growing along California's coast.

In the soft glow that lit the aquarium's passageways at night, Tristan stood staring at the giant kelp tank. It was eerily dark, and he saw little but his own reflection on the sixteen-foot-tall viewing window.

Ryder cupped his hands around his face and stuck his nose up against the clear acrylic wall. "Can't see a thing."

Pete was with them. "Ready for your next job?" he asked.

The teens nodded uncertainly.

"How about a little swim in the kelp?" asked the approaching senior kelp curator. She was carrying a bucket.

Tristan didn't think the others looked ready to dive into the inky blackness of the massive giant kelp exhibit. He wasn't so sure either. During the day, with sunlight illuminating the tank from above, the giant kelp exhibit was bright and lively. The towering, yellowy-brown seaweed resembled tall, rubbery trees with skinny stalks and long, floppy fronds for branches. And all sorts of wondrous creatures swam about, like small schools of silver sardines and silky smooth leopard sharks. But at night, the giant kelp tank reminded Tristan of a pitch-black underwater forest full of hidden creatures. It was downright creepy.

"What's the problem here?" Hugh asked nervously.

"No problem," the curator responded. "Windows just need cleaning." She handed each of the teens a soft brush from her bucket.

"I thought you had divers to do that," Rosina said grumpily.

"Oh, we do, but it will be nice to give them a break. It's a big job to keep all that acrylic clean and free of algae."

The curator led the teens behind the scenes to the top of the tank. Along with the brush, each was given a wetsuit, a small headlamp, and weights to make them neutrally buoyant. In addition, they each got a suction cup with a handle on it.

Tristan looked down into the dark water. The kelp

swayed gently due to the motion of a nearby wave machine. A small fin sliced through the water at the surface. The others turned anxiously to him.

"Leopard shark," he told them.

"It's very safe," the curator said. "Our divers go in there all the time. Nothing to worry about."

The teens each popped a rubbery, red pill into their mouths. It was the latest and most concentrated version of Sea Camp's amazing algae water. A compound from the algae strengthened their skills and gave them webbed hands and feet in the ocean.

"Glad Coach Fred gave us plenty of these," Hugh noted.

"Yeah, and since we've been using the new ones, I think I can stay underwater longer," Tristan added.

"Me too," agreed Sam.

"Yeah, and my slime is better than ever," Rosina noted, smiling sweetly at Tristan. He quickly looked away.

One at a time, the teens slipped into the water at the top of the dark kelp forest exhibit. They switched on their headlamps and sank down along the huge viewing window. The campers each chose a spot, attached the suction cup handle to the window to hold on to, and began brushing. Almost immediately, Tristan felt something graze his leg. He looked down. A three-foot-long leopard shark with black spots on its smooth, light-brown body hovered just slightly to his left. Tristan heard a voice in his head: *Yo, missed a spot over here.*

Yeah, yeah, that's real funny, Tristan thought. He brushed off a layer of fine brown fuzz, which he assumed was algae. He worked his way over to the spot the leopard shark had pointed out. The animal aimed its snout at another section of the wall. Tristan decided it was going to be a long night.

When he needed air, Tristan let go of the suction cup handle and swam to the surface. On his way back down, several other leopard sharks started to swim in tight circles around him. Tristan could hear them all talking at once. They were giving him directions on how best to clean off the algae, where to scrub, and commenting on how slow he was. It was going to be a *very* long night.

Nearby, Hugh and Rosina were having their own problems. A small school of sardines circled Hugh, while a big orange rockfish was trying to lie down on his head. Hugh kept pushing the rockfish away and it kept coming back, ready for landing. Meanwhile, a monkey-faced eel was attempting to snuggle up next to Rosina—and anyone who knew Rosina knew she wasn't exactly the snuggling type.

After about an hour of cleaning and dealing with some seriously annoying leopard sharks, Tristan thought he heard music. He stopped brushing and listened. The other teens did the same. Then Tristan heard the tune more clearly. *Dunt, dunt . . . dunt, dunt . . .*

It was the eerie theme to the movie *Jaws*. A little weirded out, Tristan swiveled around, trying to figure out where the music was coming from. When he happened to glance out the viewing window, he saw Pete laughing and motioning for them to quit working and swim to the surface.

"Couldn't resist," the communications director said as they climbed out of the tank. "Piped in the music through an underwater hydrophone. That one always gets a good reaction."

"Dude, like, *so* funny," Ryder said, trying to look cool, but clearly just as creeped out as the rest of them.

Tristan and the others took off their wetsuits, rinsed, and dried off. They then followed Pete to the sea otter exhibit. They walked by the floor-to-ceiling windows and doorway that led outside to a small amphitheater, a shallow tide pool, and the adjacent waters of Monterey Bay. It was too dark to see the kelp beds in the nearby ocean or the yellow buoys marking the intake pipes for the water that circulated through the aquarium's exhibits.

"Hope there's no rockfish on this next job," Hugh said, rubbing his head as they walked. "Besides, my fingers are already all pruney."

Pete chuckled. "Sorry about that. But since you're here for just a short time, we need to take advantage of your unusual skills."

"Cleaning windows?" Tristan asked sarcastically.

They arrived at the sea otter exhibit. It was the most popular spot in the entire place, nearly always jam-packed with people. Young and old alike plastered their faces up against the viewing window or stood five people deep just to get a glimpse of the furry creatures.

Tristan moved closer to the dimly lit exhibit. In the water were three otters floating on their backs.

Each was about three feet long, with thick chocolate-brown fur; small, dark button eyes; tiny ears; and a furry face with long whiskers and a flat, brown nose. They reminded Tristan of cuddly, buoyant teddy bears.

The sea otter tank was roughly semicircular in shape and fifteen feet deep, with a rocky back and bottom. There was also a platform at the back of the tank. Tristan moved closer to the dimly lit tank. Two otters appeared to be asleep with their front paws curled up on their chests. The other otter was grooming, using its paws to fluff up the fur on its face. Tristan had learned from the trainers that otters must continually groom their fur to keep it clean and full of air. Without the blubber of seals or whales, otters rely on a layer of air in their thick fur pelts to keep warm. Grooming is essential to their survival in the cold ocean—as is eating. To stay warm, sea otters consume huge amounts of food relative to their body size. One trainer told Tristan it was like him having to eat one hundred quarter-pounders a day. Tristan loved a good burger or two, but one hundred a day? That might be enough to make him swear off beef forever.

One of the sleeping sea otters woke up and began paddling around the tank on its back. Kicking with one foot, it zoomed about incredibly fast. The otter bumped into the wall and then crashed into another otter, waking it up. All three began doing rolling somersaults and pedaling around on their backs.

"They are too cute!" squealed Sam.

Even Rosina was taken with the otters. "Just adorable."

The boys rolled their eyes as if the otters were nothing special, though silently, Tristan agreed with the girls.

The senior trainer came out from a door next to the exhibit. "Ready to use those special powers I've heard about?"

The teens nodded tentatively.

"We've got a problem with one of the otters. See the smallest one in there? She's the one with the cream-colored fur on her face. For some reason, that little otter likes to swallow air bubbles and, well, it gives her gas."

Ryder laughed. "You mean she's got the farts?" The other teens snickered.

"I know it seems funny," said the trainer. "But it's not healthy, and she's having a hard time diving for food and getting rocks to smash open sea urchins. The purple sea urchins are her favorite."

"Uh, what do you want us to do?" Hugh asked.

"Talk to her. Explain the problem. Tell her to stop swallowing bubbles. And we need her to take this." The trainer showed them a small medicine box labeled *Instant Gas Relief*.

More giggling ensued.

"None of us have ever talked to an otter before," Tristan said, trying to keep a straight face. "Not sure if we can."

"Well, could you at least try?" the trainer asked. "Just go in there and see what happens."

"Hope it doesn't smell like sea urchin farts in there," Ryder laughed.

After several more fart jokes and a few fake burps

from Ryder, the trainer decided he was not well suited for the job. The otters could be quite sensitive. It was a small enclosure, so only two of the teens could go in. Tristan and Sam were quick to volunteer.

The two teens put on wetsuit overalls and entered the enclosure. Immediately, the curious otters turned to check out the strangers. The trainer had also given the teens a bin of enrichment feeding toys: rubber balls and cylinders filled with the otters' favorite foods (mashed-up shrimp, crab, and sea urchin). As soon as Tristan and Sam pulled out the box of toys, the otters jumped around like kids at Christmas waiting to unwrap presents. They did somersaults, dove down, and climbed over one another, all the while repeatedly popping up to stare expectantly at the pair of newcomers.

Sam and Tristan sat down on the back platform with their legs dangling in the water. They threw a few of the treat-filled toys into the water, and the otters quickly grabbed them. Tristan then offered the smallest otter a big purple sea urchin. The otter approached him tentatively. Tristan tried to communicate with it, thinking, *How about a nice, yummy sea urchin?* No response. He then tossed the sea urchin into the water. The live purple pincushion sank rapidly to the bottom. The small otter dove for it. But, about halfway down, the otter stopped abruptly. Seconds later, it bobbed buoyantly back to the surface. Another of the otters then easily dove down to snag the tasty treat. As it submerged, air bubbles released from the otter's fur rose to the surface. The small otter swam into the cloud of bubbles, opened its mouth, and swallowed.

"No wonder she's got gas," Tristan said, trying not to laugh.

"C'mon, you've got to stop doing that," Sam told the otter. Seconds later, Sam got an odd look on her face similar to when she first learned she could echolocate.

"What's wrong?" Tristan asked.

"I think I can speak otter after all," Sam told him. "The otter says she likes playing with the bubbles and the way they feel in her mouth."

"Yeah, well, explain to her why she's got to stop swallowing them," Tristan suggested.

Since they didn't need to talk out loud when communicating with sea creatures, Sam was quiet, but Tristan could tell she was concentrating.

"Where's that gas relief stuff the trainer gave us?" Sam asked.

Tristan handed her a ball filled with crab mush. "There's a pill stuck inside."

Sam tossed the crab ball to the small otter. It deftly caught the ball and quickly scarfed down the "pill à la crab." A few minutes later, a swell of bubbles erupted around the small otter. Sam and Tristan high-fived and tried not to laugh but couldn't help themselves.

"Thar she blows," Tristan said, and they laughed some more.

Looking on from outside the exhibit, Ryder, Hugh, and even Rosina were laughing. The trainer just smiled and gave them the thumbs-up.

Sam and Tristan hung out with the otters for a bit longer and then exited the exhibit. It was getting late, and they wanted to get some sleep before returning to begin their shift as regular volunteers in the morning.

Walking back to Pete's house, Tristan turned to their host. "Hey, tomorrow night's that big, fancy party at the aquarium. Right?"

"Yes."

"Guess we won't be going for a swim in any of the exhibits then," Hugh noted.

"Definitely not," Pete said, smiling.

3

RESCUED

AT THE AQUARIUM THE NEXT NIGHT, THE PRIVATE cocktail party was in full swing. Waiters in neatly creased black pants and starched white shirts roamed about, carrying platters of fancy finger food. Light jazz played over the intercom while the guests ate, drank, and explored the exhibits. A little earlier, when guests first started arriving, Tristan and the other campers had been hustled out a side door.

The teens now sat on a short concrete wall in view of the aquarium entrance. Hugh was showing the others the new mini-pocketknife tool his mother had sent. It had arrived that day at the aquarium. Hugh had told his mother during a recent phone conversation that he'd lost his other pocketknife tool earlier in the summer. He left out the part about *how* it was lost—taken from him by Marsh's thugs.

Tristan wasn't really watching or listening to Hugh. He was more interested in the arriving guests, marveling at the diversity of attendees and their varied attire. Some men had on expensive-looking dark suits. Others were dressed less formally. One guy had on jeans and a Hawaiian shirt. Another man was dressed like he was going on safari or something, clad entirely in khaki. Tristan thought he looked familiar. Many of the women were outfitted in short black dresses. A few had on long, sparkly gowns, and one lady was wrapped in a glittering sarong. A heavily bearded man then approached the entrance. He was encased in dark robes, wore a long matching scarf headdress, and was closely followed by an entourage of at least six men. When he reached the door, the man waited for one of his followers to open it. Just before he went in, the robed man turned. He stared right at Tristan—or at least it seemed that way. Tristan swiftly averted his eyes. When he looked back, the man was gone.

Just then, Pete came running out of the aquarium. He wore a wrinkled tuxedo and was breathing heavily. "There you are. I've been looking all over for you— wanted to catch you before you headed back to the house."

"Who are they?" Tristan asked, nodding to the still-arriving guests.

"Executives from aquariums and parks around the world," Pete answered. "They're here for a conference on rescue techniques and breeding for conservation, and to hear about our work to create international standards for the collecting and keeping of animals.

We work very hard and spend tons of money to make sure that our animals are well fed, live in clean water, and have enough room to swim around. But that's not true in many places in the world. Animals are kept in tiny tanks with poor water quality and fed nutrition-less junk. Two dolphins were recently rescued from a tiny pool in a theme park in Asia. It was full of murky, brown water, and the dolphins were sick, probably dying. We're really trying to prevent that sort of thing from happening, along with stopping pirate fishing and collecting."

"What's that?" Hugh asked.

"Fishing or collecting of marine life that's done ille-gally. It's a huge global issue, but don't get me started on that or we'll be here forever. About tonight—every-one's tied up at the event. So you're on your own. Okay?"

"Yeah, sure," Ryder answered, a little too quickly.

Pete eyed him and the others warily. "There's a great pizza place just down the road." He reached into his pocket and handed Sam a credit card. "Grab dinner and then head back to the house. Watch a movie or some television. Just keep a low profile—and whatever you do, stay away from the water."

"No problem, sir," Hugh told him.

"Dude, it's not like we're little kids," Ryder added. "We know how to take care of ourselves. You should have seen some of the things we did earlier this summer."

"Yeah, I've heard. That's what worries me," Pete responded. "Look, have a good night off and just don't do anything stupid." He then jogged back into the aquarium.

"Why do adults always say that?" Tristan said. "We haven't done anything stupid yet. Well, at least that I can think of."

The others shook their heads.

Tristan decided it must be a grown-up thing to worry so much. He followed the others as they walked down the road. It was their first night free and their first time without any adult supervision since arriving in Monterey. They found the pizza place and went in. It was among the many restaurants, shops, and hotels lining the road that led away from the aquarium—the famous Cannery Row. The converted sardine processing factories now hosted the trendiest places in town.

After dinner, the group began walking back to the aquarium. From there it was just a few blocks north to Pete's house. Ryder stopped and stared across the street at a small park and, beyond it, the dark waters of Monterey Bay. He raised an eyebrow mischievously. "Hey, let's go for a swim."

The other teens turned to where he was looking.

"Now? Out there? In the dark? Are you crazy?" Hugh said. "Besides, Pete said to go back to the house."

"Exactly. Like, do you always do what people tell you to?" Ryder jeered. "Are you scared, Hugh?" He turned to Tristan. "How about you? Are you afraid too, shark boy?"

"No, I'm not afraid."

"C'mon, then. Heard great whites swim around here," Ryder taunted. "I dare you."

"We've been in the ocean at night before," Tristan countered. "And it was during a *hurricane.*"

"Then it shouldn't be a problem. Or are you now *afraid of the dark*?"

The other teens watched Tristan, waiting for his response.

Hugh whispered, "Don't do it."

"Wimp!" Ryder exclaimed. "I'm going in." He jogged across the street.

Tristan hesitated but then chased after him. He could only take so much of Ryder's bluster. Besides, he didn't want the others to think he was scared or anything. With the exception of Ryder, they often looked to him for leadership. And if Tristan was going to be a good leader, he needed to be brave. Besides, he could just jump in, swim a little way out, and then get out. It was dark down by the water, so no one would see them, and if a shark came by, he'd just talk to it. He'd gotten pretty good at the swimming-fast-and-talking-to-sharks thing. What could go wrong?

The other teens followed as the two boys ran through the small park to a flight of stairs leading to a sandy beach. It was nestled between rocky outcrops at the base of a waterfront hotel and a restaurant on Cannery Row. The campers stayed in the shadows as much as possible.

As the group gathered at the ocean's edge, Ryder sat down on a rock and began taking off his sneakers. "So, who's going in?"

Hugh shook his head and glared disapprovingly at Tristan.

Tristan ignored Hugh and began to undo his laces. "C'mon. We'll just jump in, swim out, and then come back. No big deal."

Sam nodded and started to take off her shoes. "I'll go with you, Tristan."

Rosina seemed to consider joining them, but then she felt the water. "Nope, no way."

"Wuss!" Ryder announced.

"You'd better take one of these," Hugh said, handing Tristan, Ryder, and Sam each a red, rubbery pill from a plastic bag in his backpack.

Tristan and Ryder began pulling off their jeans. Rosina snickered. Sam had gone silent, obviously realizing she, too, was going to have to strip down to her underwear if she was really going in.

Minutes later, Sam, Tristan, and Ryder stood on the beach staring at the dark water, shivering. The air was cool and smelled of seaweed. Small waves lapped the shore. It was a calm night with almost no moon, even darker than usual. And except for a periodic loud laugh or the distant noise of people on Cannery Row, it was quiet.

"Chickening out?" Ryder asked.

Tristan turned to him. "No. Are you?"

"Like, no way."

Together they raced into the cold, dark water.

"I have a feeling I'm going to regret this," Sam said, before running to dive in behind them.

Almost immediately, their hands and feet became webbed. Tristan put his hands out in front of him

and zoomed ahead. He was still the fastest swimmer. But the water was so dark he could hardly see
his outstretched hands. Worried about ramming into
something headfirst at high speed, Tristan slowed. He
surfaced and stopped to look back. The beach was
already a good distance away. Tristan treaded water
and waited for the others. It was freezing compared
to the water in Florida, and his heart was hammering.
Ryder and Sam popped up nearby.

"Okay, we did it," Sam said, her teeth chattering.
"Let's go back."

"Nah, let's go farther out," Ryder insisted, staring at
Tristan in a silent dare.

"You are seriously twisted," Sam countered, starting to turn back toward shore. She paused. "Hey,
what's that?" She pointed to a dim, blue-green glow
some twenty yards farther offshore and a little to the
left.

"Let's go check it out," Ryder suggested, taking off.

Tristan and Sam looked at one another, shrugged
their shoulders, and followed. As he swam, Tristan
began to warm up. His eyes also began to adjust to the
night's darkness.

Whatever the glowing thing was, it was about ten
feet down and sort of spherical. The three teens dove
and hovered close to the shimmering orb. Tristan
watched as Sam reached out to gently touch the jellyfish's bell, staying well away from its hanging strings
of sting. The bell sparkled blue-green. As Sam pulled
her hand away, Tristan realized that it too gave off a

faint, luminous, blue-green glow. He looked at his own hands. They were shimmering too. He swam to the surface.

"What's going on with our hands?" Sam asked, staring at her glimmering hands. Then they looked at their legs, which had also begun to faintly glow blue-green.

"Whoa!" exclaimed Tristan. "We're bioluminescent."

"Awesome," Ryder added.

"Let's go back and show the others," Sam suggested. "Must be another effect of the new pills. Very cool."

"Nah, let's stay out here," Ryder said. "It's not even that cold."

"Yeah, actually, that's kinda strange," Sam noted. "We should be freezing by now without wetsuits."

"I'm liking these new pills more and more," Tristan said, thinking that in addition to now being glow-in-the-dark, the newest pills must also be why he had warmed up so quickly.

Sam ducked underwater. Tristan heard a sort of clicking noise. Seconds later, Sam popped up and pointed seaward. "The kelp is messing with my echolocation, but I think there's something out there."

Tristan squinted, trying to see where she was pointing. "Where and what kind of something?"

"Something kinda big," Sam answered. "I think it's tangled up in the kelp."

Tristan was feeling warm and more confident. "Let's go check it out." Without waiting to see what the others would say, he swam toward the forest of kelp that lay offshore. Ryder followed. Sam paused, but soon she too headed farther out into the darkness.

As Tristan got closer to the kelp, he could see that something pretty big was caught up in it, about fifteen feet down. Whatever it was, it was wrapped tight in a tangle of the rubbery seaweed and struggling to get out. Tristan dove, pushed a few pieces of kelp out of the way, and held up his hands. The faint glow from his skin provided just enough light to see what was there. But what was a *scuba diver* doing alone at night in the kelp—and without a light?

Tristan waved his hands at the diver, trying to get his attention. But the diver was too busy trying to get free of the seaweed to notice. Tristan reached out and grabbed one of the long pieces of kelp encircling the diver. The seaweed was slick and slimy, making it hard to hold onto. Tristan felt the kelp brush against his legs. He kicked at it while trying to pull at the kelp trapping the diver. Seaweed encircled Tristan's knees. Another piece began to wrap around his neck. Tristan's pulse quickened. He stopped trying to help the diver and began pushing at the kelp now wrapped around him. But his movements only seemed to make it worse. The more Tristan struggled, the more entangled he became.

Tristan twisted and turned, trying to slip free of the kelp. It wrapped tighter. On the verge of panic, Tristan felt a tap on his shoulder. He jerked around. Sam was beside him, signaling for him to calm down and stay still. Tristan forced himself to stop moving. Sam then began pulling the slick fronds of seaweed off him. Soon the kelp was loose enough for Tristan to wiggle free. He shot gratefully to the surface, where Ryder was waiting.

"Thanks," Tristan said to Sam. "There's a scuba diver down there stuck in the kelp. I tried to get him out, but started getting tangled up myself."

"I noticed," Sam said with a smirk. "What should we do?"

Ryder shook his head. "If that dude's air runs out, it's curtains. Over. He bites the big one."

"Yeah, he drowns. We get it," Sam said.

"Maybe together we can pull him up out of the kelp," Tristan suggested.

"Let's try it," Sam said. "But be careful. Don't kick or move around too much, or you'll get trapped too."

"Yeah, no joke," Tristan added.

The three teens dove down and hovered near the struggling diver. Tristan again tried unsuccessfully to get his attention. He and Ryder each then grabbed an arm. Sam took hold of the top of the diver's scuba tank. Together, Sam, Tristan, and Ryder kicked hard for the surface. The diver began to rise. They went up about two feet before the kelp sprang back like a giant rubber band, pulling them and the diver back down. The diver stopped struggling. Tristan let go and went to the surface with the others.

"Now what?" Ryder asked.

Tristan shook his head. He was thinking, wishing

his brain would come up with a brilliant idea or even a passably decent one. Nothing.

"Hey," Sam said. "Maybe we can use Hugh's new pocketknife thing to cut through the kelp."

"What?" Tristan asked.

"Dude, remember earlier? Hugh was showing us the new tool his mom sent him," Ryder said.

Since Tristan hadn't been paying attention to Hugh earlier, he just nodded like he knew what they were talking about.

"You're the fastest, Tristan," Sam noted. "Swim back and get it. We'll stay out here so you can find your way back."

Without saying another word, Tristan sprinted for shore, kicking hard. About halfway to the beach, he nearly ran face-first into a shark cruising along the coast. Both shark and human stopped short. The startled shark stared at Tristan. *Sorry*, Tristan muttered before continuing on. He then looked back at the shark, thinking about its pointed snout, big black eyes, and wide body, at least as much of it as he could see. And then he knew—it was a great white! *Wow*, Tristan thought, *I nearly had a head-on collision with a great white shark. No one will ever believe it.*

At the beach, Tristan ran from the water to where Hugh and Rosina sat anxiously waiting on some rocks. He hurriedly explained the situation out in the kelp. From his pocket, Hugh removed the mini-pocketknife tool. He handed it to Tristan, who then dove into the water and raced back toward the two specks of faint light bobbing in the kelp bed. As he swam, Tristan kept an eye out for the great white, wishing he could've at least talked to it.

Tristan, Sam, and Ryder dove down to again try to free the diver. Staying calm and moving as little as possible, Tristan opened the small knife blade in Hugh's tool. He then quickly began cutting through the kelp. As he sliced, Sam and Ryder carefully pulled the seaweed off the diver. Several breaths later, the diver was sufficiently de-kelped and rose to the surface. The man spit out his regulator, gasping for air. "Oh man, thanks, whoever you are. That was close."

"Who are you, and what the heck are you doing out here?" Tristan asked, thinking, *This guy is even crazier than us.*

It took a few minutes before the man could answer. "Same could be asked of you," he said, breathing hard. "And how come your skin is glowing like that, and where are your wetsuits? You must be freezing."

"Uh, yeah, we're freezing," Sam said, loudly chattering her teeth. "We, uh, were on the beach and saw you out here in trouble."

"Uh, yeah, that's it," Ryder agreed.

"Saw me? From the beach?" The man looked at them suspiciously. "Well, no matter. Just lucky my air didn't run out and that you kids swam out when you did. Thanks. Though I'm sure my team would have eventually figured out that something was wrong and come to get me."

The teens offered to help the man back to shore. He gladly accepted their assistance, especially since he'd lost a fin and was totally exhausted after his near-death-by-seaweed experience.

At the beach, Hugh and Rosina helped the man out of the water. He slumped onto the sand. Sam, Tristan, and Ryder quickly dried off with a couple of towels from their backpacks. They hurriedly put their warm clothes back on. The diver sat there staring as the teens' webbing began to slowly disappear and the odd blue-green shimmer faded from their skin.

"Who are you?" he asked. "And what are you?"

Tristan tried to change the subject. "What were you doing out there, anyway?"

The man pulled back his wetsuit hood to display a shock of silvery white hair. "I was testing something. But as you saw, I got a little caught up in the kelp."

"A little, dude?" Ryder said.

"What were you testing?" Hugh asked.

"Why do you want to know?"

Hugh looked taken aback by the man's response. "Geez, just curious."

"Yeah, well, I'm curious about those feet of yours. What's the scoop?"

Silence.

Tristan wondered how they were going to get out of this one.

After several minutes of no one saying anything, the diver introduced himself as Leo Ozdale. He then tried again to get the teens to answer his questions. They weren't talking.

"Okay, I get it. You're not going to answer," Ozdale said. "What really matters is what you did. You may have just saved my life. Thank you."

"You're welcome," Sam said.

"Yeah, no problem," Ryder added.

"Though a simple 'thank you' hardly seems enough," Ozdale told them. "How about lunch tomorrow on my boat? It's just north of here."

The teens exchanged nervous glances and again gave no response.

"Are you from around here?"

Tristan hesitated before saying, "We're volunteers at the aquarium."

"Look," Ozdale said. "I know the director of the aquarium. Just ask Maggie about me and I'm sure it will be okay for you to come out for lunch."

The teens remained quiet and wary.

"Just come out to the boat for lunch. I won't tell anyone what I saw, and if you don't want to tell me anything else, you don't have to. But come out. It's the least I can do."

"I don't know," Sam muttered.

Tristan silently agreed. It was hard to know whom to trust these days. But then again, the guy had already seen their webbed hands and feet, and newly bioluminescent skin.

"Just ask. I'm sure Maggie will agree, and she knows how to get in touch with me—*Leo Ozdale*."

"Do you need help with your gear or anything?" Tristan asked, again trying to change the subject.

"No, no," Ozdale told them, pulling a small water-proof radio from a pouch in his vest-like buoyancy compensator. "I've got people standing by. I'll be fine."

The teens hesitated and then said good-bye before walking away.

"Bye, thanks again," the man called out. "Talk to Maggie first thing and then have her call me. Lunch on my boat tomorrow!"

On the way back to Pete's house, Tristan turned to the others. "That was weird. What do you guys think?"

"I think we'd better call Director Davis," Hugh said. "That guy could tell others about us."

"Well, this is just *great*," Rosina moaned. "Someone else knows about us."

"Hey," Ryder countered. "It wasn't our fault. Like, we saved that guy. He probably would have died or been eaten by sharks or something."

At the mention of sharks eating someone, Tristan stared at Ryder like the teen had just insulted his mother.

"No offense, shark boy," Ryder added with a smirk. "But that guy would have been toast if we hadn't been there."

"Well," Rosina said, "wasn't like it was our fault earlier in the summer either. And look where that got us."

"Hiding from that creep, Rickerton," Sam said.

"And getting all the other campers mad at us," Rosina grumbled.

"C'mon, Director Davis will know what to do," Tristan told them. "Maybe this time, this Ozdale guy is one of the good guys."

He tried to say it like he meant it, but Tristan had no idea if the man really was someone they could trust.

4

JEWEL HEIST

When the teens arrived at the aquarium the next morning, the place was buzzing. It was about an hour before opening, and the staff and volunteers were scurrying around like a bunch of mice on a caffeine overdose. Tristan had no idea what was going on. He'd never seen the people there behaving so strangely. A worker came toward them as if race-walking while staring at the floor. The man ran straight into Hugh.

"Hey, watch it," Hugh mumbled.

"Sorry," the man said, hardly stopping.

"Like, dude, what the heck is going on?" Ryder shouted after him.

The man looked back and yelled, "Haven't you heard? A lady lost a diamond earring at the party last night. Supposed to be worth a ton. Everyone's been ordered to search for it before we open. And there's a reward for whoever finds the earring."

"Whoa," Hugh said.

Ryder peered at the ground and began to walk away. "I wonder how much the reward is?"

Tristan thought for a moment, glanced around, and then turned to Hugh. "Are you thinking what I'm thinking?"

Hugh nodded, smiling. "Let's go check it out."

The two of them took off at a run. Sam sprinted after them.

"Wait," Rosina yelled. "Where are you going?" She then ran after the others. And when Ryder saw all the other campers take off, he followed.

The teens passed the giant kelp tank. It looked a lot less creepy with sunlight streaming in from above. They rounded a corner and skidded to a stop in front of a large, square tank. A giant red, fish-eating anemone with waving, white tentacles sat attached to a rock at the exhibit's center. To the left was a cluster of fluffy, white snowflake anemones, and at the bottom, near the viewing wall, were two very big pink sea stars. The tank's main attraction, however, was mostly hidden from view. Just the tips of its two long red arms were visible, stuck to the viewing window by big white suction cups. The giant Pacific octopus was asleep in its hole.

"You think the octopus took the earring?" Sam asked.

Hugh leaned in close, scanning the tank. "Remember his little habit of borrowing things after dark?"

"Yeah," Sam said. "But I thought you said he had reformed—that he wouldn't steal anymore."

Tristan had his nose up against the viewing window. "Maybe it's a hard habit to break. I bet it's in there."

Sam pointed to the fluffy, white anemones. "Hey, look at this."

Two of the anemones were stretched out with their white tentacles extended into the water. The other anemone's tentacles were retracted, and its stomach bulged as if it had just eaten a supersized meal.

"In there?" Tristan questioned.

"Only one way to find out," Hugh said, turning to Rosina.

"I'm not going in there with that monster octopus," Rosina responded. "Hugh, you go in."

"I'm not sticking my hand into that anemone through those tentacles."

"No," Rosina said. "I meant just go in and ask the octopus."

"Oh," Hugh responded. "I can do that."

They went through a nearby door that led behind the exhibits. At the giant octopus tank, Tristan and Ryder quietly worked to remove the cover. Hugh then leaned over into the water. Tristan could tell he was concentrating. He wondered how Hugh was going to politely wake the creature and then accuse it of being a jewel thief.

"So, what's he say, dude?" Ryder questioned.

Hugh stood up. "Says he has an alibi, was asleep all night."

Sam rolled her eyes. "C'mon, Hugh, we're not

stupid. Octopus are nocturnal. They're more active at night. Tell him we're not buying it."

Hugh leaned into the tank again. Less than a minute later, he stood back up. "Now he says he was busy straightening up his tank."

Sam nudged Hugh. "Tell him we know where he hid the earring." She pointed to the bulging anemone.

The giant Pacific octopus's huge head slithered out of its hole, and it turned an eye toward the teens. Tristan swore if an octopus could look guilty, this one had "thief" written all over its giant red head. The octopus then held up its arms so that the tips were out of the water, as if saying, *See, nothing here.*

Tristan counted the arms and whispered to Hugh.

"Let's see number eight," Hugh said out loud.

The octopus paused and then lifted its other arm out of the water. Dangling from the tip was a teardrop-shaped earring with a glittering diamond as big as a marble.

"Wicked!" Tristan exclaimed. "No wonder everyone's freaked out. That thing's humongous."

Hugh gently took the earring from the octopus. "Says the earring was laying on the floor after the party. And that it was pretty."

"An eight-armed diamond heist," Tristan laughed.

"Talk about sticky fingers. Oh, I mean sticky arms," Sam giggled.

"Hey!" Hugh said. "The octopus swears the earring was lost, and he just happened to be the one to find it."

They said good-bye, and Hugh promised the octopus he'd try to put a good spin on things. They went straight to the aquarium director's office. The door was open, but they knocked anyway.

"Come in," Dr. Maggie Earle said from behind her desk. "Oh, it's you. Perfect timing. Just got off the phone with someone about all of you. Heard about your little escapade in the bay last night. What were you thinking going out there in the dark? You could have been seen. And weren't you cold?"

The aquarium director was an older woman, wearing a stylish black-and-white knit jacket. Her reddish-brown hair was pulled neatly back in a bun. Though her words and tone were reprimanding, her eyes shone with compassion and curiosity.

Hugh held up the diamond earring. "We found the missing earring!"

"Oh, thank the lord," the woman said, letting out a sigh of relief. "Where was it?"

"Uh, the giant octopus spotted it last night on the floor and picked it up," Hugh told her. "He was just waiting for someone to come by the tank this morning."

The director eyed Hugh and the other teens a little suspiciously. "Really?"

"Yes, ma'am," Hugh said. "And we heard there's a reward for finding it?"

"You want the reward?"

Hugh shook his head. "No, not for us. For the octopus."

"The octopus?"

"Yes, ma'am."

The woman chuckled. "We'll feed it an extra helping of big, juicy lobster for lunch. And speaking of
lunch, Mr. Ozdale would like to know if you are going
out to his yacht."

"His yacht?" Tristan asked.

"Yes, his yacht," Dr. Earle answered. "Mr. Ozdale is
a fine patron of the aquarium, a longtime supporter,
and quite the successful entrepreneur."

"Really?" Tristan blurted out. "We just thought he
was some crazy dude out diving in the kelp."

"We didn't mean for him to see us or anything,"
Sam said rapidly. "But he was all tangled in the kelp
and it was dark. We couldn't just leave him. I mean, he
could have died. We know we weren't supposed to go
in the water. But there he was. And—"

Hugh interrupted Sam. "We called Director Davis
at Sea Camp last night after it happened and everything."

"Yes, and what did Mr. Davis say?"

"He said he'd make some calls and that we should
talk to you."

"Quite right," the aquarium director responded. "I
think your secrets will be safe with Leo. He's a strong
supporter of the ocean and marine life. I also have a
feeling he'll be quite excited to hear about your special skills, and, who knows, knowing someone like him
might just come in handy some day. Besides, he has
some fun toys on his yacht that I think you'll all enjoy."

Tristan wondered what type of toys she was referring to. It's not like they were little kids anymore, looking to play with dump trucks or dolls.

"So, it's settled," Dr. Earle said. "Meet out at the dock behind the aquarium just before noon. One of the staff will show you where it is. A skiff from Mr. Ozdale's yacht will be there to pick you up. And by the way, let's not have any more little swims in the bay after dark."

The teens thanked the aquarium director and assured her that it had been their first and very last nighttime swim in the kelp. They left the office and made their way to their assigned touch tanks for the morning.

On the way, Ryder puffed out his chest and said, "See, nothing bad happened. Lucky I suggested we go out there. We saved that guy."

Tristan didn't say anything. He wasn't so sure what had happened was such a good thing. Sure, they had saved this Leo Ozdale guy. That was good. But now he knew about them and could blab to who knows who. Was he really someone they could trust with their secrets? Or had they just made the biggest, stupidest mistake of their young lives?

5

HOVERCRAFT TWISTER

A FEW HOURS LATER, THE CAMPERS WERE CLIMB-
ing into a small powerboat tied up at the aquarium
dock. The driver introduced herself as Sophie, one of
Mr. Ozdale's crew. She was in her early twenties and
wore dark, sporty sunglasses, a baseball cap pulled low
over her face, and a tan, long-sleeved shirt with "Super
Green" printed across the front. Tristan wondered if
the shirt meant she was a die-hard vegetarian like the
blacktip shark he helped back at camp.

The boat cruised slowly away from shore toward
the kelp beds. Tristan stared at the floppy, brown
fronds of seaweed draped across the sea surface. He
decided that kelp was definitely more pleasant when
viewed from a boat and in daylight, rather than when
all tangled up in it in the dark. He'd take a pass on

doing that again anytime soon. They neared a raft of sea otters, and Sophie slowed the boat. Tristan counted fifteen of the cute, furry creatures. Some were asleep doing the otter back float, wrapped in a blanket of kelp; others were grooming their fur as if scrubbing to lather up in a bath. Two otters popped up to stare at the passing boat. Sam waved. Tristan wondered if she knew what they were thinking. Sophie then maneuvered the boat into the open water of Monterey Bay. She pushed the throttle forward, and soon they were speeding along the coast.

From his cushioned seat, Ryder shouted, "Where's the boat?"

Over the roar of the engine, it was hard to hear anything, so Sophie just pointed north.

Since arriving in Monterey, there had been little time for the campers to play tourists and see anything except the area right around the aquarium. Tristan now stared curiously at the passing coastline. A road snaked along the winding shore. He could see an adjacent narrow walking trail lined with dark-green and red-tipped bushes. Behind it rose hills with rows of tightly packed, small homes in assorted colors.

They cruised by a small, sandy cove nestled between rocky headlands. Inside the cove, where the kelp grew thick, the water was calm and smooth. Outside, waves breaking against blocky, tan rocks created swirls of foamy, white water and spray. Tristan noticed a distinct smell in the air: salty ocean and seaweed mixed with the scent of pine.

They passed another rocky point. It was carpeted with dark bushes and topped by a single tall pine tree. For some reason, it reminded Tristan of a cherry on a piled-high ice cream sundae. His stomach growled noisily. Suddenly, just about everything reminded him of food. Hauled out on the rocks, the sleeping harbor seals made him think of big, fat, silvery sausages. The passing kelp beds became long, dark noodles in a bowl of chicken soup. Tristan hoped that eating on Ozdale's yacht didn't mean they'd be served fancy finger food like what he'd seen at the aquarium party. A big bowl of macaroni and cheese would suit him just fine. Come to think of it, the sand here was tinged a bit orange, like the gooey goodness oozing out of a grilled cheese sandwich. Tristan—and his stomach—hoped it wasn't a long ride to Ozdale's yacht.

Before long, the dense development of Monterey gave way to a winding scrub- and rock-covered coast backed by pine forests. A heavy, cool mist blanketed the shore.

Sophie slowed the boat. "This is part of the marine reserve and park."

They rounded another rugged headland and entered a small, secluded cove. Floating at the center, tied up to a mooring ball and shrouded in mist, was a large, strange-looking yacht.

"What kind of boat is that?" Rosina asked.

"That's Mr. Ozdale's eco-yacht, *Super Green*," Sophie answered proudly.

As they got closer, Tristan stared at the vessel. It

looked like something out of a spy thriller—a platform the villain used as a base of operations while attempting to take over the world or, if that didn't work, wreak global destruction. The ship was sleek, silvery-white, and nearly two hundred feet long. The stern, or back of the ship, was a raised arch between two hulls, like a catamaran. From there, the ship narrowed, curving smoothly toward the bow, which was a slightly rounded single hull. The shape of the bow reminded Tristan of a shark's snout. Three stories tall, the yacht's superstructure had tinted windows along its length. Several antennas and two giant white balls sat atop the yacht, along with what looked like solar panels curved to fit the roof.

Sophie slowed the skiff and pulled up beside the yacht's stern. "Could one of you toss up the bow line?"

Being the closest, Sam threw the rope to another crew member standing by.

"Got it," the young man said. He was dressed like Sophie and looked about the same age. Once the boat was tied up, he helped the teens climb aboard but said little. As Tristan was leaving the skiff, he noticed its name on the side: *Little Green.*

Sophie jumped expertly off the boat. "Right this way. Mr. Ozdale is expecting you."

She led them from the stern up to an open deck. Ozdale was just walking out from the yacht's interior. The first thing Tristan noticed was his cane. It was made of a light-silver, highly polished metal and undulated from thick to thin, almost like a wave, along its length. Tristan had never seen such a cane. It looked more like a shiny piece of modern sculpture. Ozdale leaned lightly on the cane as he strode forward with ungainly steps. Overall, he looked very different from the last time they'd seen him—when he'd been covered from head to toe in black neoprene, dripping wet, exhausted, and slumped on the sand. Ozdale now wore a simple white long-sleeved polo shirt and navy shorts. He was wiry thin, and his silver-gray hair was swept back as if blown by the wind. His face seemed rather ordinary, except for his eyes, which shone with a fiery glint. In general, the man definitely didn't fit Tristan's stereotype of a yacht owner. Then again, the two other yacht owners he'd met had been evil total nutjobs. It wasn't really a great pool of people for comparison.

Just then, a big dog leapt out from behind Ozdale. It stopped and stared at the teens. Tristan and the others froze immediately. The dog was black with patches of brown on its broad chest and had a pointed muzzle. Its ears were floppy and its tail just a short nub. The dog was built like a missile on legs. Tristan recognized the breed—Doberman pinscher, a well-known guard dog with teeth that could tear you apart in seconds. A low growl emanated from the Doberman, and its lips pulled back in a teeth-baring snarl. No one moved.

"Stop that, Damien," Ozdale said, chuckling.

Tristan looked at the man like he had a few marbles loose. After all, being about to be torn to pieces by a vicious dog was not something to laugh about. The dog stopped growling and cocked his head to the side.

"He's just playing," Ozdale told them. "Damien here knows that when people see him, they immediately think 'mean attack dog,' so he loves to ham it up."

The teens still didn't move a muscle.

The Doberman then leapt up like a puppy, licked the man's hand, and wagged his little tail heartily. Before any of them could even breathe a sigh of relief or think to move, the dog bounded toward them. Tristan, Ryder, and Sam dove to the side, but Hugh and Rosina just stood there, frozen. The dog jumped onto Hugh, knocking him to the ground. But instead of using Hugh as a human chew toy, as Tristan expected, the Doberman slobbered wet dog tongue all over Hugh's face.

"Damien—*come!*" Ozdale ordered.

The dog immediately leapt off Hugh, went to the man's side, and sat obediently.

Hugh rubbed the dog drool off his face. "Yuck!"

Tristan couldn't help but laugh.

Ozdale went to Hugh, bent down, and helped the boy up. "Sorry about that. We don't have guests all that often, and he just loves company."

"I could do with a little less love," Hugh noted.

"Welcome aboard," Ozdale said. "Should I call you 'campers'?"

The teens smiled nervously.

"Oh, relax," he said. "I had a lovely conversation with your Director Davis." He glanced at the two crew members standing off to the side and whispered, "Don't worry; your secrets are safe with me—and

Damien, of course." He patted the dog's head. "Come on inside."

As they walked past, the Doberman sniffed each of them as if performing a security check. Ozdale led them through a sliding double door into a wide sitting room. It was stunning in a minimalist sort of way. Cream-colored couches and several modernistic silver-frame chairs were arranged next to small, matching tables. Atop the shiny wood floor lay soft, white throw rugs.

Ozdale stopped, leaned on his cane, and waved with a flourish. "I'm very proud of the ship. The furniture and rugs are all made from recycled materials, and the decking is sustainably grown bamboo." He strode through the room to a steep stairway and turned to the group following him. "I'm a little slow on the stairs today; the old knees are not what they used to be."

They climbed slowly up the narrow stairs after Ozdale. The dog followed. On the next deck up, Ozdale headed for a long dining table. Behind it was a semicircle of floor-to-ceiling windows. Tristan imagined that, without the mist, the view would be spectacular.

Ozdale stopped at the head of the table and waved to a nearby chair. "Damien, if you would, please?"

The Doberman promptly trotted over, bent down, put his teeth gently around a leg of the chair, and pulled it out. Tristan was impressed. He wondered what else the dog could do.

"Thank you," Ozdale said to the Doberman. "Well, have a seat."

Tristan wasn't sure if the man was talking to them or the dog. Ozdale then sat down and waved to the other chairs around the table. Damien lay down beside Ozdale's chair, and Tristan took a seat. His attention was quickly drawn to the compass rose at the center of the bamboo table. It was an inlay made of varying shades of blue and green sea glass.

"I've asked my crew to serve us and then give us some privacy so we can talk," Ozdale announced. "Afterward, I thought you all might like a tour of the ship and to see some of my inventions. Maybe even go for a little ride."

Two new crew, dressed similarly to Sophie, entered the room and laid several platters on the table. As they left, Ozdale thanked them and then said, "Dig in!"

Tristan smiled gratefully. The food wasn't minimalistic or fancy, just trays of juicy burgers, creamy potato salad, French fries, and best of all, a heaping bowl of gooey macaroni and cheese. The smell was enough to make Tristan drool. He wiped his mouth just in case as his stomach made an outrageously loud rumbling noise. Beside him, Sam giggled and passed him the tray of burgers, whispering, "I think you need one of these."

Ozdale waved his hands at the food. "Didn't know what you all might like, so I had the steward whip up a selection of some of the basic food groups."

"Thanks," Sam said as they passed the platters around.

"What sort of things do you invent?" Hugh asked

before shoving a big forkful of potato salad into his mouth.

Ozdale turned to Hugh. "I bet you are Hugh Haverford. Mr. Davis said you're good with technology and have a way with cephalopods."

Hugh chewed and nodded.

"And let's see," he added, turning to the others. "You must be Tristan, Sam, Rosina, and Ryder." He'd gotten them all right.

The teens looked a little surprised.

"Mr. Davis described you all quite well and told me what each of you can do. Very cool! He also told me about Sea Camp and what goes on there. Wish I'd been invited to go when I was your age."

The teens continued eating, saying little. Tristan watched and listened to the man, trying to figure the guy out. Was he smart or a serious kook? And most importantly, could they trust him? Ozdale seemed to take no notice of Tristan's scrutiny or the teens' lack of conversation.

"As for my inventions," Ozdale went on, "they vary, but I am very interested in alternative-energy vehicles, ocean exploration, and rescue technology."

"What were you doing last night?" Hugh asked.

"Oh, that. I was testing out a new solar-powered dive light and a handheld propeller. Thought the light would last a lot longer than it did—obviously. And gosh, that darn propeller got me a bit twisted up in the kelp." The man grinned self-deprecatingly at the teens. "Guess I'll need to do a little more work on those."

"And maybe bring a backup light," Sam suggested.

"And a dive buddy," Tristan added.

"That too," Ozdale chuckled. "Sometimes I get so wrapped up in my inventions, I sort of forget the basics. My crew usually keeps an eye on things, but I don't like them hovering around too close. Ruins my creativity and the adventure of it all. Besides, they understand that I believe that failure is a good thing."

Yeah, except when it kills you, Tristan said silently to himself.

"How's that?" Hugh asked.

"Failing means I've tried something new, put myself out there. What's that saying? No risk, no reward. Failing is just part of the process toward success. Perseverance is an extremely important part of being an inventor. In fact, it's pretty important in life in general. And besides, we all learn from our mistakes."

Tristan thought about what Ozdale said. Could failure and making mistakes be a good thing? Really? He'd failed at a lot of things back home—in school, in sports. Maybe he was on his way to great success. Or not. Tristan couldn't really imagine that he'd ever invent something brilliant or do anything truly great. Though stopping Marsh and freeing the sharks in the British Virgin Islands had been pretty awesome.

The crew came in to clear the plates and deliver dessert—a giant dark-chocolate cake. When one of the crew lifted the burger tray from the table, Damien sat up, cocked his head, and stared at him. Two burgers remained uneaten. The young man looked to Ozdale, who nodded, smiling.

"Watch this," Ozdale told them.

The young man took the beef patties from the buns and tossed them into the air like two Frisbees thrown in rapid succession. Damien leapt gracefully into the air to catch one patty and then the other. He gobbled them down in seconds. The teens clapped. The Doberman sat down and stared at the burger thrower expectantly.

"You want the buns too?"

The young man then tossed the tops and bottoms of the buns as if playing rapid-fire catch. All were neatly snatched out of the air and devoured in a few bites. Damien licked his lips and happily lay back down. The young man smiled, bowed to the dog, and left the room.

While the teens each worked on consuming a large piece of cake that oozed gooey chocolate, Ozdale leaned in closer, his voice barely above a whisper. "So, how do the pills work? What about that glowing skin thing?"

Feeling a little more comfortable with the man, or because his brain was in chocolate-cake-coma mode, Tristan answered, "Don't really know how the pills work. It has something to do with algae. And we just started glowing last night."

"Interesting," Ozdale said. He rose from his chair. "C'mon, let me show you around a bit, and then we can check out a few of my creations." The man turned and, even with the cane, strode away like a giddy kid dying to show off a new toy. Damien lazily got up and turned to the teens as if asking if they were coming. The dog then followed Ozdale.

Tristan ate his last bite of cake and turned to Hugh and Sam with a questioning look. They shrugged in response. No one seemed quite sure what to make of Leo Ozdale. They eventually got up and followed the man. Ozdale started the tour of the yacht on the bridge. It had all the latest in nautical technology. The ship's electronic navigation charts and thrusters were connected to the Global Positioning System (GPS). This enabled the yacht to turn on a dime or stay precisely positioned—no matter the conditions. There was advanced radar, satellite weather imagery, and even instruments that measured ocean currents under the ship and wave height out in front. Ozdale then showed the teens the yacht's plush staterooms and led them to where he kept his collection of inventions.

Ryder immediately headed for an unusual-looking surfboard. "What's this?"

Ozdale and the others followed.

"That's my solar-powered paddleboard. It has two small propellers in a compartment inside the back of the board that can be lowered and turned on with a wireless control on a modified paddle."

Ryder gave it a cool head nod. "Awesome."

Next to the paddleboard sat a large duffle bag; a basketball-sized shiny, white plastic container; a short, thick fraying piece of rope; and something that looked like a cross between a life jacket and a parachute.

"What are these?" Tristan asked curiously.

Ozdale grinned broadly. "These are some of the new rescue technologies I'm working on. For one thing, I'm reinventing the stuffy old life raft. I, for one, never want to be stuck drifting about in the ocean with no fresh water, little shade, meager rations, and, especially, no propulsion or information on which way to go. I'm also working on ways to safely get off a skyscraper or cruise ship in case of a fire. Both projects are very hush-hush right now because I'm waiting on patents, but preliminary testing has gone well."

Tristan wondered what "gone well" meant in Ozdale's failure-is-good world.

"Except for this, of course." Ozdale picked up the beat-up piece of rope.

Given the tattered look of the rope, Tristan figured whatever it was part of had failed—in the bad kind of way.

Ozdale shook the rope and Damien bounded over, grabbed it in his teeth, and began pulling. The dog growled menacingly like when they first arrived. "It's one of Damien's favorite toys."

"What's this?" Hugh asked, standing next to something that resembled an enormous metallic egg with wings.

Ozdale walked over. "This one's been a real brain buster. Eventually, it's going to be a submersible, able to fly down to the ocean's deepest depths. I'm using a special titanium alloy hull to withstand the tremendous pressure, but still working on the controls, view, and propulsion. How about going out for a spin?"

"In *that*?" Ryder asked.

"Oh, not in this," Ozdale replied. "In my hovercraft. Do you have your driver's licenses yet?"

The teens shook their heads. Tristan wasn't sure if

he was joking or really thought that thirteen-year-olds could have driver's licenses.

"Well, no matter," Ozdale chuckled. "Not sure they even give out hovercraft licenses. That's one test I would probably fail."

The teens looked at one another questioningly.

Ozdale patted the dog on the head. "Sorry, Damien, old boy, you'll have to sit this one out. It'll be a tight squeeze as it is."

The dog lay down but watched as the man instructed his crew to open the doors at the yacht's stern. Ozdale then waved the teens over to a vehicle that resembled a small silvery-white spaceship with a skirt. The hovercraft was about the size and shape of an inflated sports car. Its front sloped down like a car's hood, and the roof angled sleekly back to an aerodynamic wing. A band of tinted, curved windows wrapped around its midsection. Painted across the vehicle's side was *Mini Green*.

Damien trotted over, and Ozdale handed the dog his cane. The man then crouched down to squeeze in through the hovercraft's small door. He turned to Sam. "How about being my copilot?"

Sam happily accepted the offer and joined Ozdale up front. The others climbed in behind them. The two rows of three seats were indeed a tight fit.

Once the teens were all inside and seated, Ozdale pressed a button. "Here we go!"

Tristan heard a soft whirring noise. The hovercraft lifted off the deck, raised on a cushion of air. The vehicle tipped to the right and then swung slightly left.

Ozdale leaned over to Sam. "Still getting the hang of it."

Raising her eyebrows over slightly alarmed eyes, Sam turned to the others. Tristan looked for a seat belt. The scooped plastic seats were seat-belt-free. Had Ozdale forgotten to include them? Maybe it was one of those basic things he mentioned often neglecting.

Ozdale grabbed hold of a joystick and nudged it forward. The hovercraft twirled slightly and then jumped forward. They moved in fits and starts toward the yacht's stern, where a large door had opened. Tristan decided either the joystick was a bit sticky or Ozdale's maneuvering abilities were also still in the "testing phase." When they reached the stern exit, the vehicle hit the side and bounced back into the yacht. Through the hovercraft's windows, Tristan saw Sophie standing nearby, shaking her head. *That can't be good,* he thought. Would Ozdale's hovercraft actually *hover,* or even float on the water, if they actually made it through the opening? He looked for an emergency exit in case the thing sank.

It took Ozdale three more attempts to get the hovercraft cleanly through the stern exit. It then slid down a smooth ramp. As they hit the water, Tristan held his breath. Fortunately, the thing really did float. He looked out and saw that they were under the arched hull at the back of the yacht.

"Now we'll just give her a little more power and take her for a spin," Ozdale announced happily. He again pressed a button on top of the joystick, and the hovercraft rose off the water. It spun slightly to the right and began to tilt sharply. The teens grabbed on to whatever they could. Ozdale pushed the joystick forward and the hovercraft leapt ahead. Seconds later, the vehicle jerked to a stop, throwing them all forward.

"Still need to make a few adjustments," Ozdale said all too merrily. "Let's try that again." Before anyone could object, he again pushed the joystick forward. The hovercraft sped ahead more smoothly this time, skimming over the water's surface. Out the windows, Tristan could see spray being kicked up around them. He started to relax as Ozdale drove more steadily.

"Yahoo!" Ozdale shouted gleefully. He yanked the joystick to the right. But instead of turning to the right, they went into a rapid right-hand spin. The hovercraft began doing 360s, twirling in place like the nauseating teacup rides at an amusement park. Rosina and Hugh went green. Ryder grabbed his seat and tried to smile like he was having fun. Tristan thought Ryder's smile looked more like a get-me-out-of-here grimace. Tristan didn't feel so good either. Luckily, before it got any worse and that macaroni and cheese made an unsightly reappearance, Sam reached out and grabbed the joystick. She pulled it straight and they stopped spinning.

"Thanks," Ozdale said dizzily to Sam. "Guess I'm still getting the kinks out. You want to take her for a spin?"

The teens in back didn't look too happy at the mention of the word "spin."

"Sure!" Sam responded. With a lobster fisherman for a father, Sam was very comfortable in boats. Though the hovercraft wasn't exactly a boat, she handled it like a pro. They were quickly zooming across the water and circling the yacht.

Ozdale grinned broadly. "Well, I know who should be my hovercraft driver from now on."

Sam giggled, clearly having fun. After she came to a stop, Ozdale offered to let the others try their hand at the helm. Hugh and Rosina declined the offer, while Ryder and Tristan wanted to give it a go. Now they just had to switch seats in the small hovercraft. It was like playing Twister in the back of a cramped floating sports car. Limbs had to be contorted and bodies entwined in exceptionally embarrassing ways. At one point, Rosina somehow managed to end up sitting in Tristan's lap. She smiled shyly at him and he laughed super awkwardly, turning at least two shades of red. Hugh thoroughly enjoyed the moment.

"Well, are you guys coming up here or what?" Sam asked, glaring at Rosina. "And don't think either of you are going to sit in *my* lap."

Ryder was the first to make it up front. His turn at the joystick, however, was short-lived. He started out okay, but then he decided to jump a small wave and nearly flipped the thing. Tristan managed to steer the hovercraft fairly straight, and even did a nice circle, before nearly decapitating them all by almost running into the yacht's anchor line. Ozdale then asked Sam to take over and drive the vehicle back up the ramp into the yacht. After another game of hovercraft Twister,

Sam steered them cleanly through the stern opening. The Doberman was pacing the deck when they arrived, as if anxiously awaiting their safe return. Tristan wondered if the dog knew something they didn't.

As Ozdale exited the hovercraft, Damien brought the man his silver cane. Ozdale leaned on it and stood up slowly. With the dog at his side, Ozdale then led the teens to what looked like a cross between a one-person airplane and a motorcycle. "Here's my latest underwater scooter design. It's still in the experimental phase. Anyone want to give her a whirl?"

Tristan could swear the dog was shaking his head at them. He and the other campers quickly declined the offer.

"Maybe another time," the man said. "Besides, I should probably be getting you back to the aquarium."

Before boarding the skiff for the ride back, the teens thanked Ozdale for lunch and the ride in the hovercraft. After a playful growl from Damien, the teens each patted him. In return, the dog provided each of them with a slimy handful of slobber.

"And don't worry," Ozdale said quietly. "Your secrets are safe with me."

The mist along the coast had thickened and spread south, so Sophie cruised back more slowly.

"Did you have a good visit?" she asked.

"Uh-huh," they answered.

"A bit of a character, isn't he?"

"Yeah, like, that dude is crazy," Ryder offered.

"How did he, you know, get so rich?" Hugh asked curiously.

Sophie smiled. "I know he's a bit of a goofball. Loves his inventions—even if they do break down or go wrong half the time—and that dog. But he's a genius when it comes to software and computer codes. He's written code for some of the biggest companies out there, and the government hires him for special projects."

"Really?" Tristan asked in astonishment. He figured the man had probably just inherited his wealth and spent his time tinkering on his "toys" or something. But according to Sophie, Ozdale was an IT genius. Tristan thought, *Guess you never can tell.*

When the campers arrived back at the dock, Dr. Earle was waiting for them. "Just got word. Time to go home."

The teens looked shocked.

"Mr. Davis says that your friend, Mr. Rickerton, is nearly in the authorities' hands."

"Nearly?" Hugh asked nervously.

"From what I understand, his US assets have been frozen," the aquarium director explained. "And they have a good lead on his whereabouts. The authorities expect to have him in custody any day. Everyone thinks it is safe for you to return home. Besides, school will be starting soon. We've made arrangements for you all to leave as soon as possible. Head back to Pete's house and pack your bags."

Tristan wasn't sure what to think. Was Rickerton

really about to be captured? The man was even slimier than Rosina's mucus. Tristan also wasn't sure he was ready to go home. It would be good to see his family and sleep in his own bed, but it also meant he wouldn't see Hugh and Sam again until next summer. And no communicating with sharks or rays, or swimming fast. Tristan had wanted to stay at least long enough to see what other talents the newest red pills might bring out, besides being glow-in-the-dark. As they headed back to Pete's house, Tristan tried not to think about how far away next summer seemed.

6

GONE MISSING

Five months later, Tristan was at home in Florida, trying to keep up at school, do his chores, and not get grounded. He missed his friends from camp and wished summer wasn't still so far off.

Meanwhile, off a small island in the Caribbean, two men stood in shallow water, staring into the distance. The shore appeared as just a thin green line on the horizon. The water was about waist deep and amazingly clear. Bright white sand covered the bottom. For now, they were alone. Their boat was the only one there, but in about an hour or so, the place would be a mob scene.

Ozdale turned to the other man. "So, where are they?"

The ruggedly good-looking man beside him

responded, "They'll be here any second. Faster if we put some fish in the water."

The two men reached into a bucket in the back of their boat, which was anchored nearby. They each pulled out a handful of cut-up fish and tossed it into the water. Almost immediately, their quarry arrived like a squadron of dark undersea stealth fighters. The creatures soared gracefully through the water. They were flat, disc-shaped, dark gray on top, and snowy white underneath. The squadron of stingrays split, with a few going left and others circling right.

Ozdale stood in awe. One stingray, nearly three feet across, passed close by. He reached out to touch it. A crowd of stingrays gathered around the other man. They swirled about him, bumping against his legs and back. The man grabbed a piece of fish and curled his hand tightly around it. He then lowered his fish-holding fist into the water. A large gray stingray with a thin black border swam onto the man's hand. The man moved his fist around in the water. The stingray followed like a twirling circle of dark-gray pizza dough. The man opened his hand and, instantly, the piece of fish was devoured.

All around Ozdale, the stingrays consumed bits of fish like a swarm of super-sucking vacuums. He grabbed some cut-up fish and began to hand-feed the stingrays. He grinned from ear to ear as they gently mauled him, searching for food. When one giant ray climbed up his back, Ozdale nearly fell over. "This is fantastic! I love this place!"

The other man did not look as happy. He was still feeding the rays, but he stared into the water, concern creasing his brow.

"What's wrong?" Ozdale asked.

"There should be at least three times as many rays as this. Earlier this summer we counted nearly seventy-five."

Ozdale spun around, trying to count the stingrays that were either swimming or lying nearby in the sand. "I see only about twenty or so."

"That's what worries me," the man said. "There should be many more."

"Maybe they're just not here today," Ozdale offered.

"Unlikely. They never miss the chance for free food. Something's wrong."

"Like what?" Ozdale asked.

"I'm not sure."

"Has this happened before?"

"Never," answered the man.

"Could they have been caught by some fishermen?" Ozdale questioned. "Do people eat stingrays?"

"People will consume just about anything. But since last March, stingrays and sharks are fully protected here in Grand Cayman. And here at Stingray City, rays may not even be picked up out of the water. That's not to say someone couldn't have taken them illegally."

"Or maybe they migrated somewhere," Ozdale suggested.

The man shook his head. "I don't think so. I'll ask

around to see if anyone has seen or heard something. It's a very small island, and people here love to talk. If only we could ask the stingrays exactly what happened and why so many rays are missing."

Ozdale was quiet for a moment and then said, "Hmmm . . . just so happens I may know someone who might be able to help with that."

The other man stared at Ozdale like he definitely had a screw loose—maybe more than one.

7

WANTED: STINGRAY TRANSLATOR

TRISTAN SAT IN HIS BEDROOM, ATTEMPTING TO DO his math homework. Christmas was a little more than a week away, and his parents had promised to take him to the beach during the upcoming school vacation. He was having a hard time focusing on arithmetic when all he could think about was zooming through the sea atop a shark. Not that he'd actually get to ride a shark when they went to one of Sarasota's beaches. In fact, his parents hadn't even said he could go in the water. Ever since they'd learned about his secret skills, they'd banned him from going into the ocean in public, afraid of what might happen. But still, just thinking about going to the beach made him imagine once again riding a shark-mobile. A knock on the door brought him back to reality.

"Tristan," his father called out. "Can we come in?"

Tristan opened the door. His mother had on shorts and her favorite purple tie-dyed T-shirt that looked as if a bunch of plums had exploded on it. She nervously ran a hand through her tousled, short, brown hair. Tristan recognized her expression. It was somewhere between motherly concern and certain horror. He'd seen it several times when he talked about camp and what went on there. And he hadn't even told her everything. Tristan's father, still dressed in his gym clothes, was trying to look equally serious. But Tristan thought he saw a hint of a smile on his dad's face. After two summers at camp and with nothing really bad happening (as far as his parents knew), his dad had become more supportive, maybe even a little jealous.

"Just got off the phone with Director Davis," his father said.

"Really?" Tristan responded. "Is something wrong?"

"No, no. But he's received a request from that man you met in Monterey last summer—the one with the fancy yacht. Leo somebody."

"Leo Ozdale," Tristan provided.

"That's it. He's asked for Sea Camp's help, specifically from you, and he's asked for your friends too."

"From me?"

"That's what Director Davis said."

"What for?" Tristan asked excitedly. He could hardly believe it. Someone asked for him specifically. That was a first. "Does he want us to go back to California?"

Tristan's mother moved closer to her son. "Now,

honey, remember, campers don't have to go on these so-called missions. We won't think any less of you if you say no. And I've got all sorts of fun planned for next week. Baking cookies, decorating the tree, fun with Aunt Ida and Uncle Joe."

Tristan tried not to stare at his mother like she just asked which was better, jumping into a pit of hot tar or eating ice cream. Did she think cookies and visiting with his aunt and uncle could possibly compare with going on a mission with his Sea Camp friends to help the ocean and save sea creatures? Besides, he hated how Aunt Ida pinched his cheeks and spoke baby talk to him. "Are you kidding? Of course I want to go. No offense, Mom."

Tristan's father broke into a small grin. "Thought that would be your answer."

His mother glared at her husband until he added, "I mean, are you sure? You'll have to miss the last two days of school before vacation."

"Definitely."

His father gave Tristan's shoulder an approving squeeze. "Director Davis said that Mr. Ozdale is on his yacht in Grand Cayman and would like you to join him there."

"Grand Cayman. Cool!" Tristan said. "Uh, where is that?"

"It's in the Caribbean, just north of Jamaica, I believe," his father answered.

"Why does he want our help?"

"He said it has something to do with a place down there called Stingray City. He wasn't very specific but assured us it's nothing dangerous—some sort of scientific investigation. But since you can communicate with rays, Mr. Ozdale asked for you."

"Awesome."

The following day, Tristan's parents drove him to Miami to meet up with Director Davis. From there, the director would take Tristan and the other teens to Sea Camp to board an airplane for Grand Cayman. During the drive to Miami, his mother had attempted several more times, unsuccessfully, to convince Tristan not to go. Tristan tried to contain his enthusiasm, not wanting to hurt her feelings. His father said little, but Tristan could tell he was proud of him. Since last summer, his dad had been hinting that he'd like to go to camp or on a mission. He even suggested that maybe the whole family could meet up during a mission. Tristan was mortified. Talk about embarrassing—having his parents show up during a Sea Camp mission. He'd be laughed out of the Conch Café. Tristan had come up with as many reasons as he could think of as to why his family should not, in any way, show up during a mission.

As they were nearing Miami, Tristan told his mother he'd probably be back in time for Christmas. He hoped he could do both the mission and Christmas. Of course, he really had no idea when he'd be back, since he had no idea what they'd actually be doing in Grand Cayman. But Tristan could hardly wait to see his friends from camp, dive into the ocean, and hopefully have a chance to once again ride a shark.

8

ISLAND VOODOO?

Tristan didn't think their Grand Cayman disguises would fool anyone; they were pretty lame. The T-shirts with *Seaside High School Debate Team* written across the front in very big letters were Coach Fred's idea. Tristan, Hugh, Ryder, Sam, and Rosina, along with Coach Fred and Ms. Sanchez, all wore the bright lime-green shirts. Tristan prayed no one would test his debating skills. He was 100 percent sure he didn't have any. Besides, with Coach Fred's military style; stocky, bull-like body; and dark hair slicked back into a stubby ponytail, the man hardly looked like a master of articulate and clever wordplay. On the other hand, Ms. Sanchez could probably pass for a hip English teacher and debate coach. Her short, slender frame; square, slightly shaded glasses; and spiky gray-

white hair made her look like an aging, intellectual
hipster.

The flight to the island had been uneventful. After
landing, a government official quietly shuttled the
group through immigration and customs. A nonde-
script white van was waiting for them outside the
airport. As the teens climbed in, Tristan immediately
noticed the steering wheel. It was on the wrong side.
The official handed the keys to Coach Fred. "There's
a map up front with directions to Sunset House—and
remember to drive on the left. We're really trying to
cut down on the number of accidents due to tourists
driving on the wrong side of the road."

Ms. Sanchez swiftly swiped the keys from Coach.
"I'll take these. I've seen you drive on the *right*." She
lithely hopped into the driver's seat before Coach Fred
could object. "Fine by me," he said. "Besides, navigation is another one of my many talents."

The teens rolled their eyes at the man's infinite lack
of modesty.

The van pulled out of the airport. Suddenly, there
were headlights heading straight for them.

"Left! Go left!" the teens shouted from the back.

Ms. Sanchez swerved into the left-hand lane.
"Oops."

Tristan decided it was going to be one scary van
ride to their hotel. He prayed it would be short.

Coach turned to the teens with his hands in the air.
"It's not too late. I could still drive."

"Oh, stop it," Ms. Sanchez said. "Just get back to
navigating and tell me where to go."

Shrouded by night, the island of Grand Cayman was pretty much hidden from view. They drove along a two-lane highway before turning onto a narrower and less well-lit road. It snaked along the coast, passing a few small hotels, clusters of palm trees, and some homes. Tristan noticed mostly that the island seemed very flat. His and the other teens' attention was focused primarily on the road ahead and keeping Ms. Sanchez on the left-hand side. Every time she veered even slightly to the right, they shouted to go left. When the van turned into Sunset House's driveway and came to a stop, the campers bailed out thankfully.

"Here we are, safe and sound," Ms. Sanchez said. "No problem."

"Yeah, like, right. No problem," Ryder groaned. "Except for us almost being killed several times."

"It wasn't that bad, Jones," Coach responded. "Just a few near misses. Now wait here while we check in."

Tristan looked around. The small parking lot was lined with tropical plants and situated between several peach-colored two-story buildings. Past the driveway and parking area, he could see a wide thatched-roof hut with people milling around. It looked like a waterfront bar or restaurant. Tristan glanced up. A cluster of coconut head-bonkers hung worryingly low from the palm tree overhead. He stepped out from under the tree.

Coach Fred and Ms. Sanchez returned with several keys.

"Jones, Hunt, and Haverford in one room," Coach said. "Marten and Gonzales, you're in another. Since we had dinner on the plane, no reason for you all to roam around tonight. Unpack and get a good night's sleep. We're having breakfast on Mr. Ozdale's yacht first thing tomorrow. We'll meet out here in the parking lot at 7:00 a.m. sharp. Have your swimsuits on and be ready to go. Oh, and we'll be by in a little while to make sure everyone is in bed and no one has decided to go for a little *nighttime swim.*"

Several of the teens glanced at Ryder. He whispered, "What?"

"Good night," Ms. Sanchez told them, handing one key to Sam and another to Hugh.

The rooms were clean, comfortable, and overlooked the ocean. Poster-sized underwater photographs of sea creatures hung on the walls. Tristan could hear waves lapping against the shore, but he couldn't see anything in the dark. He bet they'd have a great view once the sun came up. Their room had two beds and a couch with a pullout mattress. While Tristan was staring off into the night, Hugh and Ryder claimed the beds. He was stuck with the couch. As Ryder turned on the television, there was a knock on the door.

"Lights out in half an hour, boys," Coach Fred yelled through the door. "And don't try to slip out later or anything. They didn't used to call me 'eagle eye' for nothing."

Tristan shook his head. Hugh rolled his eyes, and Ryder sauntered about the room with his chest puffed out, doing his best Coach Fred impression. Tristan and Hugh covered their mouths to muffle their laughter.

Before turning off the light next to his bed, Hugh turned to Tristan. "Wonder if we'll get to use any of Ozdale's inventions while we're here."

"If so, hope they've been fully tested and he's *not* driving," Tristan responded.

Early the next morning, Tristan and the other teens stumbled, half asleep, behind Coach Fred and Ms. Sanchez. The group headed toward a small concrete dock built on the rocky shore behind the hotel. Sophie was already there, waiting for them in the skiff *Little Green*. It was early enough that only a few workers were up and about. The other hotel guests were still asleep in their rooms or having breakfast. The resort's red-shirted dive guides were preparing for the day and watched curiously as the group climbed aboard the boat.

Sophie slowly backed the skiff out. "Welcome to Grand Cayman, guys. You're lucky. Sunset House is a great place to stay, especially for divers. People can go out on boats or hop in right here. Just offshore there's a coral reef, wall drop-off, and even a mermaid—statue, that is. Divers love to have their photo taken with the mermaid. The local tourist submarine even swings by every afternoon to get a look at her."

Turning the boat north to cruise along the coast, Sophie continued, "Up ahead, that's George Town—

Grand Cayman's main town and harbor. And there's *Super Green,* moored just south of town." She pointed to Ozdale's yacht in the distance. "With the easterly winds this time of the year, the water on this side of the island is nice and calm; makes for a great anchorage."

Barely awake, Tristan hardly heard what Sophie was saying. He stared past Ozdale's yacht toward the town. Small, brightly colored two-story buildings lined the waterfront. He noticed a nearby pier with several giant cranes on it, and anchored offshore was a large cargo ship. Tristan then saw a huge white cruise ship heading toward the harbor. Soon Sophie was bringing them alongside Ozdale's sleek, silvery-white yacht.

"Nice lines," Coach Fred said, examining the ship's smooth, curving hull.

"A beauty," Ms. Sanchez added.

After climbing aboard, the group followed Sophie up a deck and through the ship to the room with the tall, curved windows. From behind a bar at the front of the dining room came a low, throaty growl. Sophie continued casually across the room. Everyone else froze. Coach Fred and Ms. Sanchez stood statue still and glanced around nervously. The growling got louder and more vicious sounding.

"Damien, you're not fooling us this time," Sam said, chuckling as she jogged toward the corner of the bar.

Coach Fred and Ms. Sanchez reacted instantly, reaching out to grab the girl and stop her. The large Doberman then leapt out from behind the bar. The dog jumped onto Sam and began to smother her with its long, slobbery tongue. Tristan laughed. Coach Fred tried to look nonchalant, as if he hadn't, seconds earlier, thought Sam was about to be ripped to shreds.

"They've got you figured out, boy," said a grinning Ozdale. He was already seated at the long dining table, enjoying breakfast. As the group approached, he stood up, knocked a glass of water over, and nearly dumped his plate onto his lap. "Welcome, campers. So glad you could make it."

One of the crew quickly came in and mopped up the spilled water as if it was an everyday occurrence. Coach Fred and Ms. Sanchez introduced themselves. Ozdale vigorously shook their hands and thanked them for coming.

After the group sat down, Damien retrieved Ozdale's napkin and placed it on his lap. Menus were passed out, along with a selection of freshly squeezed juices. While they were ordering, another guest entered the room. The man looked like he stepped out of the pages of an outdoors magazine. He was notably fit, with windswept blond hair, and wore a lightweight tan button-down shirt with a colorful image of a jumping marlin over the pocket.

"Welcome, welcome," said Ozdale, popping up from his seat and bumping the table in the process. Everyone grabbed for his or her glass to prevent a mass spillage event. Unfortunately, when Tristan reached for his glass, he knocked it over instead. The crew was right there to mop up the spill. Ozdale smiled at Tristan and gave him an I-know-what-it-feels-like thumbs-up. Tristan felt a sudden fondness for the man, a compatriot in klutziness.

"So glad you could make it," Ozdale said to the newcomer. "Campers, this is Guy Hartley, in case you didn't recognize him. Our resident celebrity." He pointed to a beautiful painting of three gracefully swimming stingrays on the wall. "That's one of his right there. Appropriate, given why you're here."

"Hi, thanks for coming," Hartley said as he sat in one of the empty seats at the table. "It's a pleasure to meet you."

Ozdale sat down as well, and Damien again retrieved his napkin.

"So what exactly is the problem at this Stingray City?" Coach asked, getting right down to business as usual.

"Do you all know about Stingray City?" Ozdale asked excitedly. Without actually waiting for an answer, he continued, "It's fantastic, been a real boon to tourism here." He turned to Hartley. "May I?"

The man nodded and smiled at the teens, clearly appreciating Ozdale's enthusiasm. As Ozdale began talking, their food was served.

"For years here in Grand Cayman, after a long day of fishing out in the open ocean, fishermen brought their boats through a cut in the barrier reef into North Sound. That's a big bay on the north side of the island. Once inside the sound, they'd break out the beer and clean their fish. You know, dump all the guts and stuff into the water. Well, it turns out that their fish waste was yummy food for stingrays. Soon lots of stingrays started regularly showing up for a free meal. A couple of divers then decided to try feeding the rays by hand. And *voila*! Stingray City was born. Dozens of rays now come to that very same spot to get fed by hand. And they're super friendly. Hundreds of people go out every day to feed them!"

"What about the sharp barb on their tails?" Hugh questioned.

"Like, yeah, dude, I heard that if you get stuck, it's bad," Ryder added.

Rosina's eyes got wide, but she remained silent. Tristan suddenly realized how quiet she'd been. She was already at Sea Camp when they arrived with Director Davis. Since then, she'd hardly spoken or even smiled at him. Not that he missed her attention or anything, but it seemed weird. He wondered what was going on with her.

Ozdale turned to Hartley. "Oh, I'm not sure about the barb."

"They only use that if they're harassed," Hartley told them. "It's a defensive tool. Hasn't ever been an issue at Stingray City."

"So what's the problem?" Coach Fred asked, trying to get back to the matter at hand.

"Some of the stingrays have gone missing," Ozdale told them. "It's a real mystery."

"You see, every year we do a survey of the stingrays," Hartley added. "We do a count and tag them to better understand and follow the population, its health, and to identify any impacts the visitors are having. This summer we counted seventy-five rays."

"Wow, that's a lot," Sam said.

"Yes," Hartley responded. "But since about a week ago, only twenty to thirty are showing up each day."

"Could some of the stingrays have gone somewhere else?" Ms. Sanchez asked.

"Doubtful," Hartley answered.

"Maybe they're just not hungry?" Ryder said.

"Unlikely. They're always hungry. Those stingrays will eat what seems like impossible amounts and then come back for more."

"Maybe some fishermen caught them," Hugh suggested.

Hartley nodded. "That's one possibility. I've asked around to see if anyone saw or heard something about the missing stingrays. Rumors about what happened are running wild across the island. Some people say fishermen took the rays, cut their meat into small circles, and sold them as scallops. Others say the stingrays were caught to use as bait for bigger fish. One man insists he's seen some big tiger sharks in the area and thinks they've been eating the stingrays, or at least chasing them away. It's also been suggested that climate change, the moon, or even island voodoo are responsible for the disappearance of the rays. So far, there's no evidence to support any of the theories— especially that island voodoo thing."

"That's why we called you," Ozdale jumped in again. "Nobody can figure it out. Oh, and I asked Director

Davis, and he said it would be okay if I told Guy here about your, you know, special skills." He winked at them. "So we thought that Tristan, with your particular talents in communication, you could go out there and question the rays that are left. Maybe you can find out what really happened."

Everyone in the room turned to stare at Tristan. He had just shoved a giant forkful of pancakes into his mouth, so he just nodded enthusiastically.

"Sounds like a plan," Coach said. "When can we go?"

"How about now?" Hartley responded. "We want to get out there before all the tourists arrive. I've got a boat on the north side of the island and can take you from there. It'll be much quicker than going from here."

"Eat up, campers," Coach Fred announced. "We've got work to do."

9

STINGRAY CITY

When they arrived at the marina, Ozdale and Hartley were waiting in a twenty-two-foot power-boat tied to a dock. To get there from Sunset House, it had taken only about fifteen minutes, two wrong turns, and one scary driving-on-the-wrong-side-of-the-road incident. Tristan half expected Damien to be there too, but Ozdale must have left the dog on the yacht, along with his silver cane.

"Hop on in," Ozdale said with childlike eagerness.

"Do you need any special equipment or anything?" Hartley asked.

"That's a negative," Coach answered.

The teens, Ms. Sanchez, and Coach Fred climbed into the boat. It had a small roofed center steering console and two large outboard engines. A couple of coolers sat in the back, along with a bucket. The adults stood behind the steering console while the teens sat on benches in front of it and along the sides of the boat.

Tristan breathed a sigh of relief when Hartley took the wheel, glad that Ozdale wasn't driving. Hartley turned the key and the engines roared to life. "Ready to cast off."

Coach Fred released the stern line, and Sam jumped up to get the rope at the bow.

"This is so exciting," Ozdale gushed.

Coach Fred rolled his eyes at the man.

Hartley steered the boat away from the dock. Tristan noticed the red mangroves lining the other side of the canal. The plants' crooked orangey roots hung down into the olive-colored water. They motored slowly from one canal into another, passing other boats, more mangroves, and a development of homes surrounded by lush gardens. One tree caught Tristan's attention. It was tall, bushy on top, and crested with flaming-orange flowers. Exiting the system of canals, they entered the broad, open bay known as North Sound. An easterly breeze created a small chop on the bay's light-green water.

Hartley pushed the throttle forward. "Hang on."

The boat sped offshore. With a deep V-shaped hull and powerful engines, it planed fast and smooth over the small waves. Tristan smiled as the wind whipped his face and the water rushed by. He loved racing across the water and being on a mission with his friends. And so far it seemed like a pretty simple, no-crazy-wackos kind of investigation. He glanced back to the fading shoreline. The low-lying island wrapped around to both the right and left, while ahead lay only open water. Tristan glanced over at Rosina. She had her head down and was staring glumly at her feet. She wasn't the most cheery person even in the best of circumstances, but now she seemed almost on the verge of tears. Again, Tristan wondered what was going on with her. Maybe Sam or Hugh knew. He'd have to remember to ask them.

Some fifteen minutes later, they slowed. Tristan stood up and stared ahead. The water was now crystal clear and so turquoise it looked artificial, like someone had poured food coloring into the ocean. And the sand was dazzling white. *No wonder people liked this spot,* Tristan thought, *even without the stingrays.*

Hartley coasted the boat to a stop and hit a button to release the anchor. The boat drifted backward as a short length of chain, and then rope, spooled out. Once the anchor was firmly set, Hartley cut the engines. "We probably have a good half hour before the tour operators start showing up," he told them. "There are actually two spots that make up Stingray City. This is called the sand bar, for obvious reasons. It's pretty shallow, about two to four feet deep depending on the tide and wind. It gets the biggest crowds. Just to the west of here is a deeper spot, nearer to the barrier reef—where those waves are breaking farther offshore. That's where divers go and this whole thing started. We'll start here. Then, if there's time, we can hit the other spot later."

"Excellent," Coach Fred said as he turned and nodded to Ms. Sanchez. From a small backpack, she pulled out a plastic bag half-filled with algae-water pills. She gave each of the teens a pill, along with some water from one of the coolers. Hartley and Ozdale watched curiously.

"How long do they take to work?" Ozdale asked.

"It's really fast once we get in the water," Sam answered.

"What exactly do they do?" Hartley asked.

"You'll see," Coach replied. "Now, Tristan, we want you to question the rays about what happened. Where are the missing stingrays? Who did it? Did they see anything? When did—"

"Got it, Coach," Tristan interrupted. "But where are the . . ."

Before Tristan could get that last word out, he saw something moving in the water about twenty-five feet from the boat. It looked like a swirling dark cloud heading their way.

"Sometimes just the sound of the boat attracts them," Hartley noted.

The swarm of sleek gray stingrays cruised silently to the boat and began circling. Tristan could swear some were more than four feet across. Everyone leaned over to stare at the stingrays.

"The big, darker ones are the females," Hartley told them. "The smaller, light-gray rays are the males."

Tristan watched as one of the big females swam toward the boat. It resembled a big, dark disc with two raised eyes on top and a short, whip-like tail. He couldn't see the barb. Just before hitting the boat, the stingray swerved, flashing its creamy-white underbelly.

Hartley opened one of the coolers and removed a bag of cut-up fish. "Lionfish," he said. "Speared them out on the reef the other day. Nasty invaders here and throughout the Caribbean. But these southern stingrays really love 'em—if *we* kill 'em and cut 'em up ahead of time."

"We've cooked lionfish on the yacht," Ozdale added. "Pretty good once you get past the poisonous spines."

"Yeah, I cut those off first thing."

Tristan peered into the clear, shallow water around the boat. He counted twenty-five stingrays circling. The idea of jumping in with so many rays was exciting and a little scary, though Tristan would never say that out loud. He prayed the rays would talk to him. It would be megamortifying if he and the others came all this way and then . . . nothing. *Nah*, he thought to himself, *don't worry*. Of course they'd talk to him. He was good at this stuff.

Hugh leaned over to watch the creatures cruise around the boat. "Little kids get in with them, right?"

"Oh, they're perfectly harmless," Ozdale responded. "Watch."

The man slipped off his shirt and slid slowly, but excitedly, into the water. The stingrays immediately swarmed around him. They swam by his legs and bumped into him. Ozdale laughed like a kid.

"Jump in," Hartley said, encouraging the teens.

Ryder slid into the water. Tristan followed and Sam after that. Hugh and Rosina remained in the boat.

"Whoa!" Tristan exclaimed as a huge, three-foot-wide stingray collided with his leg and slipped past.

Its white underside was silky smooth against his skin. A small light-gray ray then cruised over his foot, and another ray bumped into his stomach, nearly knocking him over. Tristan hopped around, trying not to step on any of the stingrays. And all the while, in his head, he heard the rays: *Hey, mon, where's the food? Feed me! Give it up* . . .

Tristan started laughing as more rays collided with him while others swam close by. Ryder twirled around as two rays circled him.

Sam grinned as she bent down to pet a passing ray. "This is so cool."

Coach yelled down to Tristan, "Hunt, what are they saying?"

Tristan looked up. "They're too hungry and obsessed with getting food to answer any questions. I think we better feed them first."

Hartley jumped in with them. "Just watch your fingers. They can be a little enthusiastic."

"Uh, sir?" Hugh asked from the boat. "What exactly does 'a little enthusiastic' mean in stingray terms?"

Tristan had been wondering the exact same thing.

Ms. Sanchez laughed. "Yeah, those big females could probably suck a snail right out of its shell!"

"Well, let's just say it's best to mind your fingers," Hartley told them. "Here, watch." He grabbed a piece of lionfish from the bucket now sitting in the very back of the boat. Curling his fingers tightly around the fish, he lowered his hand into the water. A large stingray was on him in a flash. It cruised over and nuzzled his hand. "Their mouths are underneath. See—if I move my hand around, it will follow."

The ray followed, staying on top of the man's hand, doing the dark twirling-pizza-dough routine. "When you open your hand, do it quickly." Hartley swiftly uncurled his fingers and the stingray instantly sucked up the fish. He turned to the others in the water and held out some fish for them to take. "Want to give it a try?"

Tristan nervously took a piece of fish and tightly curled his fingers around it. The stingrays were swimming all around him. He slowly submerged his fish-holding hand. A huge dark-gray ray with ridges along its back slid onto his hand. Tristan stayed very still and watched the ray. He felt its soft, smooth underside and its mouth on his hand. Mimicking what he'd seen Hartley do, Tristan then slowly swung his hand around underwater, keeping his fingers curled tight. The ray followed. Using his other hand, Tristan stroked the top of the creature's disc-shaped body. It felt very different than its soft underside—slightly bumpy and a little rough. Not wanting to tease the stingray, Tristan quickly released his fingers. The ray vacuumed up the fish super fast. Tristan smiled and laughed. He loved Stingray City. He turned to see what the others were doing.

Ozdale was playing with two of the rays and feeding them hunks of lionfish. Ryder was teasing a small gray stingray by moving his fist, which was curled around a piece of fish, swiftly through the water in different directions. After a few minutes, presumably tired of

Ryder's game, the ray swam off. Ryder opened his hand to entice the ray back. It raced in and grabbed the fish.

"*Oww!*" Ryder yelped. "The thing bit me." He held up his hand. There was a tiny nick on one of his fingers.

"Oh, poor baby," Rosina teased from the boat.

Tristan looked up at her. Rosina wasn't exactly smiling, but at least she wasn't about to cry or anything now.

Of course, as soon as Ryder put his hand back in the ocean, his amazing healing abilities kicked in. In seconds, the small cut on his finger was gone.

Tristan heard Sam laughing and turned to see what was so funny. She was having a hard time staying upright. She was the smallest in the group, and the big rays kept playfully knocking her over.

While Ozdale and Hartley encouraged Hugh and Rosina to get in and give it a try, Ms. Sanchez slid into the water, unable to resist the fun. Hugh and Rosina followed more tentatively. Coach remained all business in the boat. He stood with his hands on his hips, supervising.

Once in the water, Hugh stood very still as two rays approached. He didn't take any fish to feed them, but reached out tentatively to touch a ray as it passed. Then one bumped into his legs. Hugh smiled. The stingrays paid little attention to Rosina at first, but as soon as she put her hands in the water, five rays were all over her.

"Hey, watch it," Rosina said. "Get away. I don't have any fish."

Ms. Sanchez chuckled, petting a passing ray. "Oh, I didn't think of that."

"What?" Tristan asked, watching as Rosina twirled around trying to avoid the rays. She looked ready to jump back into the boat.

"It's her mucus," Ms. Sanchez said. "They probably like it. Think it's fish slime."

"Don't worry," Hartley told her. "They won't bite or anything. Well, except for maybe a little love nip."

"Oh, great. That's all I need," Rosina moaned as a ray nuzzled her hand. After a few minutes without any love nibbles, nips, or bites, she visibly relaxed. With a mischievous smirk, Rosina then stepped up to Ryder and patted him on the back.

"Hey! Yuck, what're you doing?" Ryder said, twisting to look at the mucus now dribbling down his back. A huge ray then bumped him, slid up onto his back, and began sucking off Rosina's slime.

"Dude, get off me!" Ryder shouted, trying to wiggle out from under the ray.

The others laughed as Ryder appeared to dance with the big stingray. Rosina headed toward Hugh, who quickly backed away. "Don't come any closer," he warned.

When the ray that had been on Ryder swam away, he again twisted his neck around to see his back. "What the—?"

A large round red welt now marked Ryder's back. It was about the size of a baseball.

"Oh," Hartley said. "I forgot to mention that they do that sometimes."

"Do what?" Tristan asked.

"Give people hickeys."

"Aargh!" Ryder shouted, before dunking underwater. He tried frantically, yet unsuccessfully, to wash off the slime-sucking stingray hickey.

The other teens, including Rosina, fell over laughing.

Even Coach Fred let out a little chuckle before saying, "Okay, okay, enough fun and games. Hunt, get to work. And Haverford, I saw some fish swimming around. Find out if they know anything."

Hugh floated on his stomach and kicked lightly to chase after some silvery fish with a yellow stripe along their midsections. Hartley and Ozdale stared wide-eyed at his webbed feet.

Since being fed, the stingrays had calmed down. Some were still cruising around the teens, looking for food, while others lay nearby on the sand. Tristan ducked underwater, trying to choose a specific ray to communicate with. A large female with black trim around her body cruised toward him. He thought, *Hi, I'm Tristan.* The ray stopped suddenly and hovered in front of him. It shook its head or the front part of its body. Tristan wasn't sure where the head ended and the body started. He heard the ray say, *Ya, mon, met a whole lot of humans out here, but no one's ever talked to us.*

Yeah, we get that sometimes, Tristan thought. *It's kinda a long story.* He then pointed at his webbed hands and feet.

Whoa, bobo! exclaimed the ray.

Tristan wondered what *bobo* meant.

That's just a local saying, the ray told him. *Like "buddy" or "pal."*

Tristan then explained that they were there to find out what happened to the missing stingrays, and asked if the ray knew anything about it. The big stingray told him to hang on and swam away. Moments later the same ray, recognizable by its dark border, came back. Next to it was a smaller light-gray stingray with a partially healed wound across its back.

He was there, mon, when it happened, the ray told Tristan.

When what happened? Tristan asked.

The other ray settled onto the sand next to where Tristan was kneeling down in the water. Its eyes turned toward him. *The bad men came and took my sister, along with a bunch of our friends.*

Who came? Who was it? Tristan asked.

Don't know, mon, the smaller ray told him. *But look at my back. I barely escaped the nets.*

Hold on, Tristan told the rays. He stood up and relayed what the ray said to the others.

"Ask them when it was," Coach said. "And if they know what happened to the rays."

Now, except for a few stingrays still swirling around Rosina, most of the rays were swimming near Tristan or laying on the sand like they were listening in on the conversation. Tristan asked them the questions. Another stingray answered, saying it was late at night and that they didn't know what happened to the missing rays.

Tristan popped up and told the others.

"Ask them if they remember anything that will help us identify who did it," Hartley suggested. "And how many rays were taken?"

Tristan chatted with the group of stingrays for a few more minutes before standing up. "They don't know exactly how many rays were captured. Some stingrays left the area and are too scared to come back. Could be as many as fifteen or twenty that were taken."

"Any idea what happened to the rays?" Ms. Sanchez questioned. "Were they fishermen who took them? Were the rays killed?"

"They don't know. But there is one stingray that might know something more. She almost got caught. Jumped right out of the boat. But they said she's pretty freaked out, traumatized by the whole thing."

"Where is she now?" Coach Fred asked.

Tristan shook his head. "That's kind of a problem. None of the stingrays have seen her since that night."

Sam floated over to Tristan and stood up. "Ask them if they know where she might be."

Tristan asked, and the rays mentioned several locations where they thought she might be hiding. Tristan relayed the information to the others. Hugh then popped up nearby, staying well away from Rosina. "Caught up with some yellowtail snappers. They said good riddance to the rays. More food for them. If they know something, they're not talking."

The noise of boat engines drew the group's attention to the south. A pontoon boat, a double-decker powerboat, and a catamaran all loaded with people were headed for Stingray City's sand bar.

"We'd better wrap this up and get you all out of the water," Coach told them.

Hartley tossed in the remaining lionfish and climbed up a small ladder at the boat's stern. He turned and put out a hand to help Ozdale climb the ladder. The others followed.

Ozdale stared at their hands and feet as they got out of the water. "Just amazing."

The teens used towels to quickly dry off and cover their webbed appendages until they were back to normal.

Hartley looked out to the reef a little to their west. A dive boat was just arriving. "I think we'd better skip the deeper site." He pulled up the anchor and they headed back to shore.

On the boat ride back, the roar of the engines was too loud for them to discuss what they'd learned. Tristan sat thinking. He had a whole lot of questions. In fact, he had more questions than answers. Why would someone take the stingrays? Were they caught by fishermen, to be killed and cut up? Did that mean the rays were all dead now? If not, where were they? Seems like it would be pretty hard to hide a bunch of giant stingrays.

10

MAD MAX AND DARTH VADER

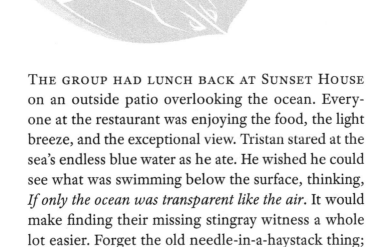

The group had lunch back at Sunset House on an outside patio overlooking the ocean. Everyone at the restaurant was enjoying the food, the light breeze, and the exceptional view. Tristan stared at the sea's endless blue water as he ate. He wished he could see what was swimming below the surface, thinking, *If only the ocean was transparent like the air.* It would make finding their missing stingray witness a whole lot easier. Forget the old needle-in-a-haystack thing; this was going to be way harder. He sure hoped the stingray was at one of the locations the other rays had mentioned.

Ozdale joined them for lunch, but Hartley couldn't make it. He had a date with a painting of a hammerhead shark that needed finishing. He had wished them

luck and asked that they keep him informed if they discovered anything new. Just before Hartley left, he gave
them the link to a Web site with data from a tracking
study of the stingrays in Grand Cayman. He thought it
might be helpful in their search.

After their plates were cleared, Coach Fred pulled
out a chart of Grand Cayman and laid it across the
table. Ms. Sanchez had gone to her room to retrieve a
laptop so they could look at the tracking data Hartley
mentioned.

"Do you think the stingrays were fished for food?"
Hugh asked.

"Do people really eat stingrays?" Sam asked,
scrunching up her nose and looking totally grossed
out.

"Probably somewhere in the world they do," Coach
answered. "People also sometimes mislabel seafood
products, secretly selling less-desirable species as fish
types that are more appealing and expensive."

"Don't let the stingrays hear you call them 'less
desirable,'" Tristan said. "I don't think they'd like it."

"Except as food," Hugh noted.

"Maybe the stingrays are still alive and being held
somewhere," Sam said hopefully.

"It's possible, but not very likely," Coach answered
bluntly.

Tristan knew Coach was probably right, but he still
wanted to believe the missing rays were alive. "Why
would someone take them, if not for food? And where
would you hide a bunch of huge stingrays?"

Just then, Ms. Sanchez returned to the table. Along with her computer, she'd brought a map for tourists that she picked up at the hotel's front desk. "I remembered seeing something on this map that I—"

"Okay, let's get to it," Coach Fred interrupted as he stared at the chart. "Hunt, where did those rays say that stingray witness might be hiding?"

Tristan thought back to what the rays had said, hoping he remembered correctly. "I think it was South Sound, Ghost Mountain, and Killer Pillar Reef."

"South Sound is down here," Ozdale told them, pointing to a small reef-enclosed lagoon on the south side of the island. "And it's not marked on the map, but I think Ghost Mountain is up here." He pointed off the coast at the northernmost tip of the island. "Ghost Mountain is a pinnacle reef. Nice dive site, but much deeper than North Sound, where the stingrays usually hang out. And Killer Pillar Reef is off George Town, south of Ghost Mountain, and shallower. Some nice stands of pillar coral, hence the name."

"Let's take a look at the tracking data," Coach said, turning to Ms. Sanchez. "That could help narrow our search variables."

"Okay, but as I was saying before—or *trying* to say," she said, giving Coach the evil eye. He shrugged in apology. "I also think there's another place we should be looking into."

"Where's that?" Ozdale asked.

"Remember Tristan's question? If the rays are alive, where would you hide them?"

Everyone nodded.

"Well, look at this," she unfolded the tourist map and pointed to a spot north of George Town. It read in big bold letters, *Oceanland: Don't dive? Don't worry. Come here to see all the creatures of the sea.*

"You think Oceanland stole the stingrays?" Tristan blurted out.

"I don't know," Ms. Sanchez offered. "But they probably have holding tanks big enough to house some stingrays."

"Roger that," Coach responded. "We'd better check it out."

Hugh was staring at the tourist map curiously. "What's this place near Oceanland? It's marked 'Hell.'"

Ozdale laughed. "Everyone visits Hell at some point. It's a hell of a place."

The others stared at him.

"It's a joke," the man told them. "Hell is the name of a tourist site where there's an outcropping of nasty-looking old blackened reef rock and a post office. You can go there and mail your friends a postcard from Hell. Get it?"

They chuckled. Tristan thought of Director Davis's love of bad jokes and puns. He'd probably love to go to Hell.

Ms. Sanchez turned on her computer and pulled up the Web site for the stingray tracking study. "Let's take a look at where Grand Cayman stingrays spend their time other than Stingray City."

The Web page had a satellite image of Grand Cayman and two groups of stingrays listed on a sidebar. Under the Stingray City group were names, including Shadow, Mad Max, Dorothy, and Toto. The other group, which was labeled *South Sound stingrays*, included Belle, Shorttail, Hoover, and Darth Vader. Ms. Sanchez clicked on Mad Max, and a curling, bright-blue line popped up on the image. She zoomed in and read from an accompanying text box, "Mad Max spends his days at Stingray City. At night he rests in the sand farther to the north or sometimes forages in the sea grass beds to the south."

They clicked on each of the rays in the Stingray City group, looked at the tracks, and read the accompanying information. Then they did the same for Darth Vader and the other stingrays in South Sound. Hugh made notes on a napkin as they studied the data.

"So let me see if I've got this right," Hugh said. "The stingrays at Stingray City spend their days getting easy handouts, and then at night most of them rest in the sand. While in South Sound, Darth Vader and the other stingrays spend their nights foraging in the sea grass and their days resting in the sand in the lagoon."

"Yes, that's what the data suggests," Ms. Sanchez confirmed.

"So if the female that jumped off the boat is hiding out with the rays in the South Sound group, during the day she's probably resting in the sand," Hugh added.

"Affirmative," Coach said. "A daytime recon of South Sound appears warranted."

"I still think we should also check out Oceanland," Ms. Sanchez said.

Coach nodded. "Roger that. We'd better split up.

If the stingrays are still alive, and that's a big *if*, time could be critical. Too much longer and they could be killed or transported someplace where we'll never find them."

Tristan didn't like either of those options.

Coach and Ms. Sanchez went to call Director Davis with an update. Tristan and the other teens walked down to the water. A dive boat was departing the dock, and a couple of snorkelers had just jumped in.

Tristan stared longingly into the clear blue water. The day was sunny and warm. Part of him wished they were just normal kids so they could jump in and go for a swim. Then again, what normal kid could ride a shark, talk to stingrays, and go on secret undersea missions? That was *way* better. He looked to the north. Ozdale's sleek yacht sat quietly in the distance. Behind it were two cruise ships now anchored offshore and the one cargo ship he'd seen before. Tristan hoped they would find the missing witness and figure out what had happened to the stingrays. And more than anything else, he prayed the rays were still alive and that they'd find them before it was too late.

11

SEARCHING FOR CLUES

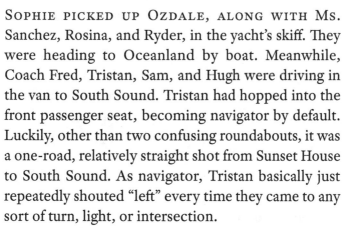

SOPHIE PICKED UP OZDALE, ALONG WITH MS. Sanchez, Rosina, and Ryder, in the yacht's skiff. They were heading to Oceanland by boat. Meanwhile, Coach Fred, Tristan, Sam, and Hugh were driving in the van to South Sound. Tristan had hopped into the front passenger seat, becoming navigator by default. Luckily, other than two confusing roundabouts, it was a one-road, relatively straight shot from Sunset House to South Sound. As navigator, Tristan basically just repeatedly shouted "left" every time they came to any sort of turn, light, or intersection.

The small parking lot and dock at South Sound were empty when they arrived. In the distance, behind a barrier reef, Tristan could see a couple of dive boats tied up to mooring balls. The lagoon was shallow, oval shaped, and about a mile long by a half mile wide. The bottom looked sandy, with scattered dark-green patches of sea grass.

"No point in me going in," Coach told them. "I'll coordinate the operation from here."

Staring at Coach Fred, Tristan suddenly realized he'd never actually seen him swim. He'd been in boats, traveled in a submersible, and yelled at them a lot from shore—but Tristan had never seen Coach actually in the water swimming. Maybe the man wasn't a very good swimmer or didn't even really like the water.

"What are you staring at, Hunt?" Coach barked.

"N-nothing, Coach," Tristan stammered.

"Now, according to that tracking data, the area where the rays seem to spend their time isn't too far out," Coach Fred told them. "I'd estimate it to be about halfway between shore and the reef." He gave each of the teens a red pill. "Now go out there and find that stingray. Make your interrogation quick, but be firm and purposeful. Don't let the creature see your fear."

Fear? thought Tristan. *What is this guy talking about?* He looked around. Didn't appear to be anything to be scared about.

"Ask detailed questions, but don't say anything more than necessary—"

"Okay, okay, Coach. We got it," Tristan said, thinking that if their line of questioning didn't work, Coach would probably suggest some form of sea-creature torture to get the ray talking. *The man really needs to chill sometimes.*

"And Haverford, don't just hang around out there. See if there are any other animals that might have seen our witness or know something."

"We got it, Coach," Hugh repeated, rolling his eyes.

Before Coach could provide any more advice or bark more orders at them, the three teens jumped off the dock and swam out into South Sound. Tristan scanned the sand and sea grass, searching for stingrays. A couple of fish resembling long-beaked, skinny silver hot dogs glided up to them. Tristan and Sam looked to Hugh, but he shook his head, signaling that they weren't talking. The teens swam farther out. Sam stopped and pointed to a large queen conch sitting on the bottom. Hugh dove down.

Tristan and Sam treaded water overhead, waiting to see if Hugh could talk to the conch. Shellfish were notoriously hard to communicate with.

"Maybe you can use your echolocation to find the rays," Tristan suggested to Sam while they waited.

"Good idea."

Hugh popped up next to them. "Nope, nothing."

Sam ducked underwater and made her dolphin-like clicking noise. She then cocked her head to the side and closed her eyes, concentrating. Back at the surface, Sam motioned for them to follow her to the right. "This way."

The two boys swam behind Sam. They kicked gently with their arms at their sides, scanning the bottom for any sign of a stingray.

Tristan saw a goatfish poking around in the sand.

Suddenly, a cloud of fine white sediment erupted from the seafloor. A stingray shot off the bottom and, quick as a whip, it was gone. Tristan popped his head up. "Awfully jumpy."

"Over this way," Sam told them. This time they swam more slowly and tried to be as quiet as possible. She led them to a sandy spot next to a patch of thick-bladed sea grass. Sam pointed to the bottom.

At first, Tristan didn't see anything. Then a little puff of sand drew his attention. A stingray, about two feet across, was lying on the bottom, almost completely buried in sediment. Tristan hovered quietly, not wanting to scare it away. He tried to think nice stingray thoughts, like: *Nice tail. Great sand you've got here. That's an excellent camouflage job you've got going.*

The stingray shifted slightly.

Hey, how's it going? Tristan added.

The skiff *Little Green* was nearing a dock on Grand Cayman's northwest coast. Two other small boats were already tied up beside the pier. Sophie expertly maneuvered the skiff in. Ozdale, Ms. Sanchez, Ryder, and Rosina then climbed out. Sophie handed Ozdale his sculpture-like cane.

"We're going to take a little tour," Ozdale told his driver. "You know, like regular tourists. And then we'll be back. Shouldn't be more than about an hour or so."

"Yes, Mr. Ozdale," Sophie responded. "I'll be here waiting."

The group made their way to the Oceanland entrance. After Ozdale paid the required fees, they wandered into the park.

"Like, where should we start?" Ryder asked.

"Yeah, where would you hide twenty giant sting-rays?" Rosina added.

"Let's just walk around like all the other tourists and try not to look suspicious," Ms. Sanchez said, glancing pointedly at Ozdale.

"Hey, I can do inconspicuous," Ozdale said.

The others looked at the man skeptically.

"Just keep an eye out for any stingrays or large hold-ing tanks," Ms. Sanchez told them.

Oceanland was a small park that catered mainly to visiting tourists. The group walked along a path that led to a large tank full of sea turtles. As soon as they arrived, nearly every sea turtle in the pool popped its head up and turned to look at the new visitors. The park's other guests stared as the animals all began swimming toward the teens.

"Walk faster," Ms. Sanchez said quietly.

"What's going on?" Ozdale asked, also staring at the sea-turtle caravan headed their way.

Ryder ducked his head and picked up his pace.

"Ryder here can communicate with sea turtles," Ms. Sanchez whispered. "And clearly they have something on their minds."

Ryder didn't wait to find out what the sea turtles

wanted to tell him. The commotion was already draw-
ing too much attention to them. He ran ahead. Next
they came to a small, winding stream lined with large
white rocks. Inside the stream swam a bunch of big
bright-blue parrotfish, a school of surgeonfish, two
nurse sharks, and a couple of large stingrays. The
group paused as one of the stingrays cruised by.

"Where's Tristan when you need him," Rosina said.

Ms. Sanchez walked to where the parrotfish seemed
to be congregating. She bent down, stuck her hand in
the stream, and closed her eyes, concentrating. "My
communication skills aren't what they used to be, particularly outside of camp's Rehab Center, but I think
they're saying they've all been here for a long time. No
newcomers. Let's move on."

On the group's left, a wall of hibiscus plants and
small palm trees gave way to a couple of tall cages. One
had a large, strange-looking iguana in it—like a miniature dinosaur that had fallen into a bucket of bright-
blue paint.

"The blue iguana is endemic to Grand Cayman,"
Ozdale told them. "It's only found here, but the species almost got wiped out—due to humans, of course.
Fortunately, through conservation efforts, the population on the island is now increasing."

In the next cage were two very odd-looking birds.
They were brown with large, astonishingly red webbed
feet and bright-blue bills.

Rosina stepped up to the enclosure and read a sign:
"Red-footed booby; native to Little Cayman."

"Little Cayman is a smaller island to the northeast of here," Ozdale told them. "Has one of the world's largest breeding populations of red-footed boobies. Kind of goofy-looking, if you ask me."

"What do our feathered friends have to say?" Ms. Sanchez asked Rosina.

Rosina squinted and focused on the birds. Then she shook her head and rolled her eyes. "They asked if we have any snacks in our pockets."

"Hey, how'd they know?" Ryder said. From his pocket, he pulled out a smashed, half-eaten sandwich filled with French fries, ketchup, and pickles. "But this is for me, not some goofy birds."

"Ugh, you're going to eat that?" Rosina moaned.

"Saved it from lunch. All this investigating mission stuff makes me hungry."

"Yeah, but that's gross."

Ryder responded with a wide grin and then shoved the half-eaten sandwich into his mouth, chewing like it was the best thing he'd ever tasted.

Ozdale laughed. "Looks pretty good to me; I'll have to try that sometime."

"But do the birds know anything about the stingrays?" Ms. Sanchez asked Rosina.

"Nope. Said they don't know anything about any missing stingrays."

The next enclosure they came to had a small island with a shallow pond around it. A large gray crocodile lay on the sand. After that was a touch tank containing two large stingrays and a school of small, golden cownose rays. People were leaning over the side to pet the rays.

The four of them gathered around the ray touch tank. Ozdale reached in to stroke a small cownose ray as it passed, and stared at the two big stingrays circling. "What do you think?"

"Hard to say, but they look like they've been here for a while," Ms. Sanchez noted. "They seem well acclimated to the tank and people petting them. I don't think these are our missing rays. Let's keep going."

The last area they came to was Oceanland's main attraction. The wide lagoon was separated from the ocean by a low rock wall. It was home to the park's two bottlenose dolphins. A stand of empty bleachers sat on one side of the lagoon. The two dolphins were swimming lazily through the water, and one was pushing a plastic football with its beak.

"Sam would hate this," Rosina said. "Seeing them captive like that."

"Yeah, and they probably have to do tricks for food," Ryder added. "Though, if the food was good, maybe that wouldn't be so bad."

"Oh, brother," Rosina responded.

"Come look at this," Ms. Sanchez said, pointing to a plaque on a nearby wall. "It says the two dolphins held here were injured in a hurricane and separated from their pod. They were brought here and rehabilitated but, due to their injuries, can't be released. And they don't do tricks for food, but trainers work with the animals on a daily basis to keep them fit and entertained."

"Oh, well that's better," Ozdale added.

Rosina and Ryder nodded in agreement.

"We strongly oppose the capture of wild dolphins or whales to put in displays or parks," Ms. Sanchez explained to Ozdale. "But if they are rescued or bred in captivity and cannot be released, the animals can be of great help to educate people and promote conservation efforts. And if the animals are well fed, well cared for, and housed in sufficient space, it's not such a bad life for them."

Ozdale nodded. "Yeah, no predators or fishing lines, lots of clean water, and all the food they can eat." He nudged Ryder playfully. "Sounds pretty good to me."

"The conditions here look good," Ms. Sanchez noted. "Sometimes animals are not so lucky. I hate to think of our ocean friends in captivity in bad conditions. Just breaks my heart."

"The ocean's animals are lucky to have someone like you looking after them," Ozdale said admiringly to Ms. Sanchez.

Ms. Sanchez smiled shyly and motioned for the group to move on. The path from the dolphin lagoon took them to a garden maze that led to the park's exit. After running up against four dead ends in the maze, Ryder cheated by hopping over a hedge. Mid-jump, something seemed to catch his eye. He climbed onto a flat-topped rock nearby and peered over the maze's hedges. "Like, check this out."

Ms. Sanchez and Ozdale stood on their tiptoes to see what Ryder was looking at. When Rosina approached the rock he was standing on, Ryder reached out a hand to her. Rosina paused and looked questioningly at the outstretched hand.

"I'm not going to bite," Ryder told her. But then he noticed a thick smear of ketchup on his hand. He rubbed it off on his shorts and stuck his hand out again to Rosina. She took it and climbed up onto the rock beside him. "Thanks."

"No problem," Ryder responded. "A little food and, really, I'm a pretty nice guy. Thought you guys would have figured that out after I came back and saved your butts in the British Virgin Islands."

Rosina rolled her eyes good-naturedly and then pointed to a bunch of big tanks in the ground a little way off behind the hedges. "Wonder what's in those."

"Exactly," Ryder said.

Ozdale followed the garden hedge to a nearly hidden wooden gate. It was locked. He glanced around to see if anyone was watching. "Might have some bum knees, but I can still do this." He put his cane on the other side of the gate and climbed over. "Let's find out what's back there."

"Oh, Mr. Ozdale," Ms. Sanchez said, looking around. "I'm not sure that's a good idea."

"It's not a good idea. It's a great idea, dude," Ryder said, scrambling over the gate as well.

"Well, while you two go see what's in those tanks," Ms. Sanchez offered, "we'll stay here on lookout in case someone comes."

Back in South Sound, Tristan had inched stealthily closer to the stingray lying nearly buried in the sand. He saw its eyes follow him. *What's up?* Tristan said, trying to sound cool and nonthreatening.

The stingray looked directly at him. *What's up?* Then it glanced upward. *Uh, water?*

No, uh, that's just kind of a greeting, Tristan thought.

Really? Well, bobo, it's a weird way of saying hello.

Tristan had never thought about it, but the stingray was right. Taken literally, it *was* kind of a strange way of saying "hello." He shrugged before explaining who they were and asking the ray if it knew anything about what happened at Stingray City.

Yeah, mon, of course I know about it. All us rays have been keep'n a low profile ever since, if you know what I mean. With that, the ray flicked its broad fins so that even more sand covered its flattened body. *Hey, what gave me away, mon?*

Tristan explained about Sam's ability to echolocate.

She don't like to eat stingrays, does she, bobo?

Definitely not, Tristan replied.

In that case, what ya wanna know?

Tristan popped up and waved Hugh and Sam over. "It says it knows about what happened and will talk to us."

While Hugh and Sam floated nearby, Tristan dove down and asked the ray what it knew. A few minutes later, the stingray shed its sandy disguise, rose from the sand, and then cruised slowly off into the distance.

Tristan went to the surface and treaded water. "It's not our missing witness. The ray said the same thing as the rays at Stingray City. Some guys with nets in a boat at night grabbed a bunch of rays."

"What about the one that got away? The witness?" Hugh asked.

"It said rumor is that she's hanging around a place called 'Cheeseburger.'"

"Cheeseburger?" Sam asked.

"That's what it said."

"Well," Sam added. "I guess that's some—" She abruptly stopped talking and twirled around as if looking for something.

"What's wrong?" Hugh asked nervously.

"I thought I heard something."

"Like what?" Tristan asked.

"Like that," Sam said, pointing to a large gray fin rising up out of the water about fifty feet away. It was moving rapidly toward them.

"Oh no, not this again," Hugh groaned, paddling so that he was behind Tristan. "Hope your shark thing is working."

Tristan ducked under, trying to see what type of shark it was.

"It's not a shark," Sam told them.

A whoosh of water hit the three teens as a large bottlenose dolphin sped by.

"Phew," Hugh sighed.

Circling back and propelled by the powerful pumping of its tail, the dolphin headed directly for them,
fast. Just before crashing into the teens, it swerved. A
wave of water sent the campers rolling backward.

Hugh righted himself, spit out seawater, and turned
to Sam. "Hey, what's it doing?"

Before Sam could answer, the dolphin returned,
and this time it slammed into Tristan, headbutting him
in the stomach. "Umph!"

"Whoa," Hugh said as Tristan again tumbled backward.

Tristan gasped for air and turned to Sam. "What
was that for?"

"Hang on, I'm trying to communicate with it," Sam
replied.

And just as she said that, the dolphin swam up to
them underwater and snapped at her toes.

"Let's get the heck out of here," Tristan urged.

"Yeah, that is one crazy dolphin," Hugh added.

But Sam didn't want to leave. She wanted to try
again to communicate with the dolphin. After it rushed
them another time, the two boys grabbed her by the
arms and pulled her toward shore. As they neared the
dock, Tristan turned to Sam. "You didn't see any mind-
control cameras or anything on that dolphin, did you?"

Sam shook her head, mystified by the dolphin's odd
and aggressive behavior.

Ozdale and Ryder crept quietly toward the group of large square tanks covered loosely with light-gray tarps. Ryder reached the first tank and lifted the cover. He said softly to the others, "Turtles."

They walked toward another of the tanks.

"Hurry!" Ms. Sanchez shouted as loudly as she dared. "I think someone's coming."

Ryder lifted the tarp over another of the tanks as Ozdale moved to one nearby.

"Everything okay, ma'am?" a man asked as he approached Ms. Sanchez and Rosina. He wore an Oceanland shirt and had a walkie-talkie on his belt.

"Oh, hello there," Ms. Sanchez said a little too loudly. She turned so that when the man looked at her, he was facing away from where Ryder and Ozdale were checking out the tanks. "Yes, yes. Just looking at these beautiful hibiscus plants. Do you know what species they are?"

Turning quickly to see whom Ms. Sanchez was talking to, Ozdale smacked his shin hard against the corner of a tank. "Yeowwy!" He hopped around, holding his leg.

"Hey!" the Oceanland security guard shouted. "What are you two doing in there? That's a restricted area. Get out of there *now*!"

Passing Ozdale, Ryder whispered, "Nice going, dude. Way to be inconspicuous."

Ozdale shrugged sheepishly and limped along behind Ryder. He leaned heavily on his shiny silver cane. At the gate, they climbed over to join the others.

Ozdale made it seem much more difficult than earlier, nearly stumbling as he climbed. And when he approached the man from Oceanland, he leaned on his cane as if it was the only thing holding him up. "Just curious, sir," Ozdale said innocently, rubbing his shin.

With his feet planted squarely apart and hands on his hips, the man stared at them suspiciously. He paused as he took in Ozdale's cane. "Well, go be curious somewhere else. You know, I could have you arrested and charged with trespassing."

"No harm done, sir," Ms. Sanchez said. "We're just on our way out."

The Oceanland employee stood firmly with his arms crossed and kept his eyes trained on the group as they headed for the park exit.

"The cane comes in handy sometimes," Ozdale whispered to them. "Use it to pull the sympathy card when needed."

Later, back on Ozdale's yacht, the two groups gathered to discuss what they'd found.

"So, what *was* in the tanks?" Coach Fred asked Ryder.

"Just some sea turtles in one and fish and a couple of sea stars in another. We didn't have time to, like, look in the rest. Someone got us kicked out." He stared accusingly at Ozdale, who shrugged apologetically.

"The guard's reaction was a bit odd," Ms. Sanchez added. "Seemed a little too harsh for some wandering tourists."

Coach looked to Ozdale. "Any idea what 'Cheeseburger' refers to?"

Ozdale pulled out the chart they'd been looking at earlier. He pointed to a spot offshore, a little south of George Town. It was labeled Cheeseburger Reef.

"So, what's our next move?" Ozdale asked enthusiastically.

"A nighttime recon of the other Oceanland tanks seems in order," Coach Fred offered. "How secure did the place look?"

Ms. Sanchez shook her head. "Coach, let's put off the breaking and entering for now. A better and *more legal* approach might be to visit this Cheeseburger Reef and see if we can find that stingray witness."

"Of course that's another way to go," Coach Fred responded disappointedly. "But let's not rule out another—more stealthy—Oceanland operation."

"What about the dolphin? And the way it was acting?" Sam asked.

"What dolphin?" Ms. Sanchez asked.

"Oh, yeah. We forgot to mention that," Coach Fred said, nodding to Sam to explain.

After she told them about the crazy attack dolphin, Ozdale laughed. It was not the reaction Tristan or the others expected.

"You had the pleasure of meeting Stinky!" Ozdale told them.

"Stinky?" Sam asked.

"Oh, he's a legend around here. Showed up some time ago, all by himself. No pod or other dolphins around. And he's got a real mean streak. Likes to harass divers and cause all sorts of mischief."

"Yeah, well I can do without his kind of mischief," Hugh said.

Tristan was just glad Stinky wasn't out to get them personally, like the mind-controlled sharks in the British Virgin Islands. Been there, done that.

"So, getting back on point," Coach Fred said. "How deep is Cheeseburger Reef? What's the layout? Is it a popular dive site?"

Ozdale answered Coach Fred's questions as best he could. The group then decided to have dinner aboard the yacht and, afterward, to make a visit to Cheeseburger Reef. At night, the daytime dive boats would be gone and they should have the place to themselves. Coach suggested that if it wasn't too late after that, they could still break into Oceanland.

12

CHEESEBURGER REEF

A SLIVERED MOON HUNG OVER THE CALM SEA, AND the hint of a breeze tickled the air. Ozdale's skiff rocked gently, tied to a mooring ball at Cheeseburger Reef. Coach Fred and Ms. Sanchez were aboard. The five campers had already slipped quietly into the sea. The thin, full-length, black wetsuits they wore concealed most of their bioluminescent skin. Ozdale had also provided each of the teens with a small solar-powered dive light, after assuring everyone that the lights had been fully tested and would last for hours.

As the campers dove down to search for the missing stingray witness, Ozdale lit the way with the headlight on his underwater scooter. He sat aboard the vehicle in a wetsuit and scuba gear, like an undersea motorcycle rider.

Ten feet below the surface, the teens came to the top of Cheeseburger Reef. In the scooter's wide, dim beam, the reef resembled a cluster of dark, mini mountains rising up from the sand. Tristan swam deeper and turned on his dive light for a better view. Humps of brown star coral topped the mini mountains. Sheets of the coral draped over the sides. There were also lumpy patches of a greenish coral, a few clumps of purple finger coral, and tangles of a thin yellow branching species. Like chains of cornflakes dyed green, strands of algae hung down from pockets in the reef. A school of small brilliant-blue fish darted through Tristan's light. Following behind were several larger black, pointy-nosed fish with fluttering fins. Tristan turned to follow the fish and nearly ran headfirst into a cluster of enormous tube sponge. The sponge reminded him of big yellow foam pipes sticking out from the reef. His light illuminated another sponge. It was vase-shaped, iridescent purple, and glowed as if lit from within. The sponge's vibrant color and glow seemed almost unreal. Tristan swam closer for a better look. Wanting to show the others, Tristan looked around to see where they were.

Ozdale hung back from the reef on his scooter, observing. Tristan thought he looked a little wobbly, and wondered how much drive time the man had on the undersea vehicle. To Tristan's right, Sam and Rosina watched a sea turtle munching on algae. Hugh was close by as well. He seemed to be having a staring contest with a large fish, which hung motionless in front of him. It was silvery-red with big eyes, a sloping forehead, and a pouty mouth. If Tristan remembered correctly, it was some kind of snapper. He didn't see Ryder but figured he was somewhere nearby too.

Tristan swam deeper. He sensed movement to his right and swung his light that way. One of the biggest, most colorful parrotfish he'd ever seen was swimming toward him. It was fat, nearly three feet long, and had huge white buckteeth. It was also half bright-green and half bright-red, with dark purplish-blue lips, as if it was wearing a funky shade of lipstick. The humongous fish reminded Tristan of a creepy undersea clown. Still watching, and a bit unnerved by the creepy clown fish, Tristan reached the sandy bottom. The coral mini mountains narrowed at each of their bases, giving each an almost giant-mushroom-like shape. A wide over-hanging ledge about a foot or two above the sand created a dark space going under and into the reef. Tristan swung his light around, noticing more holes and crevices in the reef, all of which were filled with a murky blackness.

Tristan decided to go up for air so he could explore the base of the reef further on his next dive. Returning to the bottom, he pointed his dive light into a three-foot-wide crevice. He swam into it, lured by the mysterious darkness ahead. The crack widened into a small tunnel that jogged to the left. Tristan swung his light onto the tunnel's walls. They were covered with bright-red and orange sponges. He swam slowly, going farther into the winding passageway, deeper into the reef's dark inner recesses. A curling lime-green whip of coral hung down and hit him in the face. Tristan then swerved to miss bumping into another glowing purple vase sponge sticking out from a wall. He pointed his light ahead. Two giant eyes stared back. Startled, Tristan hit his head on the tunnel's low ceiling. His heart pounded as a thick, five-foot-long silver fish cruised by. A tarpon. Tristan continued on. The tunnel now twisted to the right. He thought about turning around before he ran out of air. But the temptation to explore further was too great. After all, the inside of the reef would be an excellent hiding place for the missing stingray.

Tristan swam deeper into the reef. His chest began to tighten, signaling that soon he'd need to go up to the surface for air. *Just one more turn*, he thought. Tristan kicked a little harder. The passageway opened up into a cavern. It was filled with hundreds of silversides. Moonlight streaming down from above lit up the small silver fish as if they were under a spotlight onstage. Tristan traced the light up to a hole in the reef. It looked big enough for him to swim through. He swam into the cloud of silversides. The fish parted in nimble synchrony. Tristan's chest got tighter. Time to go up. He quickly looked around. No stingray. Tristan rose up to the hole and began to swim through. His head made it through, but then he came to an abrupt halt. His shoulders were stuck. The hole wasn't quite as big as he'd thought. Now Tristan's lungs were screaming for air. As rapidly as he could, he wiggled and twisted to get his body through the hole. Suddenly, he felt a rush of water, as if something had just raced by. Tristan popped out of the hole and swam fast for the surface. Had something gone by while he was getting out of the reef? Was it the stingray?

Tristan surfaced near the other teens. So far, no one had seen any stingrays or learned anything helpful. Hugh said the fish were jumpy and hesitant to talk. Many were in hiding. Ozdale then came up on his scooter and promptly fell off. The campers headed back down to the reef to continue their search.

Tristan swam down and around the coral. He kept his eye out for whatever might have swum by earlier. Another shelf-like overhang caught his attention. He hung upside down and pointed his dive light underneath. A small cloud of sand drifted up through the light. Tristan sank deeper, until he was lying on the bottom. He saw another puff of sand, as if something had just swum away. Tristan swam under the ledge, peering into the darkness ahead. Was something in there? He moved slowly, trying not to stir up the sand with his webbed feet. His light hit a wall of old coral. He was in a small cave—a dead end. He angled the light down and around. Just then, on the bottom and to the right, something moved. He looked closer. It was a large stingray trying to cover itself with sand. Tristan shut off his dive light to avoid a deer-in-the-headlights reaction and put his hands out, letting their dim shimmer guide his way. He kicked gently toward the stingray, again trying not to stir up the sand. *Hi, I'm Tristan. Don't be scared.*

The ray stopped moving and settled on the bottom.

Tristan thought it might be the ray they were looking for. *Hey, how's it going?*

The stingray shook a little sand off and looked up at Tristan. *Mon, you're ruinin' my cover!*

You don't need to hide from me. I'm here to help.

Hidin'? I'm not hidin'.

Tristan thought maybe it wasn't their witness after all. *Oh. Well, okay. We're looking for the ray from Stingray City that was there when the other rays were taken.*

Why you want to find her, mon?

Tristan paused. *Did I say it was a her?* he thought to himself. He looked suspiciously at the ray. *We're trying to find out what happened.*

The stingray shuffled more fully out of the sand, like it was about to make a swim for it. Tristan blocked its path. Unable to escape, the large gray disc of a creature settled back onto the seafloor. *It was bad, bobo. Really bad. That's why I'm 'ere.*

Hiding? Tristan asked.

No way, mon. I'm not hidin'. I'm on a stakeout.

What? Tristan asked.

A stakeout. Don't ya know what a stakeout is?

Of course I know what a stakeout is, Tristan thought. *But what are you staking out?*

Tristan then sensed something behind him. He turned. A nurse shark had just entered the cave. It was at least four feet long and had a flat head and small, light-colored eyes. Two whisker-like barbels hung from the shark's chin. At the side of its mouth was a thick white scar where a wound had obviously healed.

The scarred shark did a U-turn and stopped next to the ray. *Look 'ere. Is this guy bothering you? Want me or my pals to take care of him?*

Tristan tried to back up. *Hey, I'm just trying to help.*

The nurse shark proceeded to quiz Tristan about his intentions. After that, it wanted to know his background and qualifications to assist them. Tristan hurriedly tried to answer all of the shark's questions. His chest started to tighten.

The shark turned his head and stared at Tristan with one eye. *Why should we trust you?*

Tristan needed to go up to the surface. *Stay here; I'll be right back.*

Tristan bolted out of the cave and to the surface. After a quick gulp of air, he dove back down. He raced to the cave entrance and nearly ran headfirst into the nurse shark. It swerved and swam past him. The stingray was following close behind.

Hey, wait! Where are you going? What about the stakeout?

The nurse shark turned to Tristan. *Mon, you've blown our cover.* The shark then nodded up to the surface, adding, *A few of my relatives should be coming by soon. Hang here if you want, bobo. Talk to them. Then again, if they don't think you can be trusted, at least we won't have to worry about you ruining our stakeout again.* The shark opened its mouth and chomped its jaws threateningly several times.

Tristan got the not-so-subtle message. He wasn't sure he wanted to meet the nurse shark's relatives.

As the nurse shark and stingray swam off into the dark, Tristan looked around for the other campers. Not seeing anyone, he headed up. The other teens were hanging onto a line beside the boat. Ozdale had remounted his scooter and sat unsteadily nearby. Tristan headed toward them.

"Found it," Tristan yelled as he swam.

"The stingray?" Ms. Sanchez asked from the boat.

"Yup, but she's not hiding like the others thought. She's on a stakeout."

"A stakeout?" Hugh asked.

"That's what she said."

"Why a stakeout?" Rosina asked.

"That's what I asked. But I had to come up for air and then they took off."

"Who's *they*?" Coach questioned.

"A nurse shark was with the stingray. It said a couple of its relatives would be by soon and we should talk to them." Tristan decided he wouldn't mention the whole they-might-eat-you scenario.

"What kind of relatives?" Hugh asked warily.

"Those kind," Sam answered, pointing to several dorsal fins approaching the boat. The moon gave off just enough light to see their very large triangular silhouettes.

"Whoa!" Ozdale leapt off his scooter and climbed into the skiff.

The campers scrambled in as well—all except Tristan.

13

THE SHARK PACK

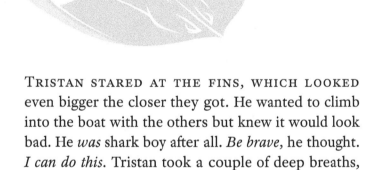

Tristan stared at the fins, which looked even bigger the closer they got. He wanted to climb into the boat with the others but knew it would look bad. He *was* shark boy after all. *Be brave,* he thought. *I can do this.* Tristan took a couple of deep breaths, trying to stay calm. Coach Fred aimed a light over the side of the boat.

"Man, they're big," Hugh said. "Must be at least fifteen feet."

"Like, they're the biggest sharks I've ever seen," Ryder added.

"Geez, thanks guys," Tristan muttered.

Tristan clung to the small dive platform at the back of the boat. He nervously ducked underwater. Coach's light illuminated the lead shark as it neared. It *was* the biggest shark he'd ever seen. And he'd seen some pretty big sharks. The one coming toward him had a huge, wide head; its big black eyes looked nearly three feet apart. The shark's dorsal fin had to be a foot high. Then Tristan saw black stripes across the shark's back. He knew what kind it was. It didn't make him feel any better. Nor did the shark's partially open mouth, which was filled with rows of dagger-sharp, serrated teeth. Tiger shark. Tristan remembered reading about tiger sharks. They reportedly ate just about anything. In their stomachs, scientists found other sharks, birds, and stingrays, along with a license plate, boots, and even a bag of potatoes. And tiger sharks were known to be especially curious, aggressive, and unpredictable. Tristan's heart pounded harder. He hoped this tiger shark wasn't feeling moody or hungry for a new snack sensation.

The shark silently cruised by, one eye staring at Tristan. It then tilted its head as if to get a better look at him or survey which of his limbs looked the meatiest. Behind the first lengthy tiger shark was another, along with five smaller blacktips. Closely following the blacktips was a group of small striped fish, like a bunch of big-shark groupies. The shark pack swam by Tristan and circled around the boat.

"What are they saying?" Sam asked.

Tristan shook his head and hung absolutely still in the water. He waited for the sharks to come back around, thinking about how to best introduce himself and make it clear that he was a very poor snack choice—low in nutrition and not very tasty. Nothing brilliant came to mind. The big tiger shark in the lead again headed toward him.

Uh, hi, Tristan thought. *I'm Tristan, and I can talk to sharks.*

The tiger shark swam by and Tristan thought it said, *Duh.*

The second tiger shark then approached. It paused to stare at the teen. Tristan decided to just get to the point, thinking, *Heard you might, uh, have some information about what happened at Stingray City.*

Who told you that?

Tristan quickly explained who they were, why they were there, and that he'd talked to the stingray and nurse shark on the reef below. The shark hovered and stared at Tristan, as if deciding whether to believe him or check out his flavor profile. It swam away, followed by the pack.

Tristan looked into the boat, thinking maybe now was a good time to get in. Then the lead tiger shark came back. *So you're looking for some information?*

We're trying to find out what happened at Stingray City.

What's it to you?

Tristan tried to relax, but the thudding of his heart was like thunder in his ears. He wondered if the shark could sense it. He kept thinking about the nurse shark's warning. He took a deep breath and again explained who they were and why they were there.

Cool yourself, said the shark. *First of all, we don't eat humans, especially skinny kids like you. And besides, you've already seen me. We eat ambush style. You know, the whole surprise-attack thing. It would ruin our reputation if we swam up, said hello, and then took a bite.*

Yeah, uh, okay, thanks, was all Tristan could think to say.

We've been cruisin' these waters for years. Come here every winter. This place is known for its excellent sea turtles. They're crunchy-good.

Tristan cringed at the thought of the shark eating a sea turtle.

Have you ever tasted sea turtle? the shark asked, knowing Tristan's thoughts.

No, Tristan answered.

Then don't knock it. Believe me, I've tried a lot of stuff. Then again, I never have tasted boy. The shark inched closer.

Backing up, Tristan speedily told the shark, *I'm sure sea turtles are great, fantastic, really.*

The shark stopped and Tristan could swear it was smiling.

Just kiddin'. I'm not going to eat you. We're here for the same reason as you. We want to know what's going on around here.

What do you mean? Tristan asked.

A lot of strange things have been happening. Fish from reefs suddenly disappearing, stingrays taken, and some of our local relatives are missing.

Is that why the stingray and shark were on a stake-out? Tristan asked.

The shark twisted its head from side to side, looking around suspiciously. *Yeah, man. Cheeseburger Reef's lost a bunch of fish and some sea turtles.*

Maybe we can work together, Tristan suggested.

The tiger shark paused and looked Tristan over, considering his offer.

Tristan suddenly felt uncomfortable as he waited to see what the shark would say. He decided maybe some small talk would help. *I live in Florida; have you ever been there? It's pretty nice. So, how come you don't have an accent like the stingrays and nurse shark? You know, the 'mon' and 'bobo' thing.*

The shark seemed to perk up a bit. *Been to Florida a couple of times. Way too many people; they scare all the fish away. And we're not full-time residents of the Caymans. Travel a lot. Guess that's why we haven't picked up the accent.*

That's cool, thought Tristan.

Look, the shark told him. *We're about to head north to check out some suspicious activity a couple of fish reported. If you really want to help figure this thing out, you can come along. Who knows, maybe you humans can even be helpful for once.*

Tristan tried not to take offense at that last remark. *Okay, thanks. Let me tell the others.*

With the skiff following slowly behind and a nervous Ozdale nearby on his scooter, the sharks led the group north. The teens, including Tristan, had decided to remain in the boat for the time being. They cruised slowly past George Town. Tristan could see the colorful holiday lights decorating the buildings and spiraling up tall palm trees. He'd nearly forgotten it was almost Christmas. Tristan wondered what his parents and sister were doing. Decorating a tree? Eating cookies? Having their cheeks pinched by Aunt Ida? *That* he would definitely not miss. But now that he thought about it, Christmas with his family was fun. He did miss his parents and even his sister—a little bit. His mom was always so funny about making sure all the ornaments on the tree were positioned just right, while his dad teased her by moving them around behind her back and seeing if she would notice. And her Christmas cookies were exceptionally tasty.

Then Tristan looked over at Hugh and Sam standing beside him in the boat. He noticed Coach Fred's determined expression and Ms. Sanchez putting a towel around Rosina to be sure she was warm. And of course there were the two giant sharks leading them north. Tristan realized there would be other Christmases with his family if he didn't make it back in time. He was in Grand Cayman and on a mission with his friends to hopefully save some stingrays and solve a mystery. That was much more important than one Christmas at home. He had a job to do!

Tristan refocused his attention on the sharks as they led them north. He wondered where they were headed. Oceanland? Then he noticed a massive, dark shape up ahead. It was the cargo ship he'd seen before, anchored offshore.

The sharks slowed and circled back to the skiff.

"Hunt, you'd better jump in and see what's going on," Coach Fred said.

"Got it, Coach." Tristan slid back into the water.

The lead tiger shark told Tristan they were headed past the cargo ship to check out the area behind it to the north. They were going to swim alongside the giant ship to hide their movement. Tristan relayed the news to the others.

Tristan then suggested it was time to go stealth shark-mobile mode. The other teens agreed. He hoped the tiger sharks would too. He ducked back underwater and politely asked the lead shark if they'd be game for a ride-along.

You want to ride on our backs? the shark asked. *That's definitely a first. Most humans swim away from us screaming.*

Tristan explained that they'd ridden on some bull sharks earlier in the summer and he thought it was the coolest, best thing ever!

Then jump right on, the shark told him.

"The sharks are up for it," Tristan told the others.

"Now, you all be careful," Ms. Sanchez told them. "If things get scary or dangerous in any way, we want you back here right away."

Coach Fred slapped Ryder on the back and then took Hugh by the shoulders and looked straight into his eyes. "This is what you've trained for. You can do it.

Go in there and figure this thing out. Oh, and if it gets really dangerous, then you can all come back, I guess."

"Thanks, Coach. I think," Hugh said as he and the other campers slid into the water.

Ozdale's eyes nearly popped out of his head when Tristan grabbed the lead tiger shark's giant dorsal fin and swung a leg over its back. Rosina was about to climb on behind Tristan, when Sam raced in and jumped on ahead of her.

"Rosina, you and Ryder go on the other shark," Sam told her firmly. "Hugh, climb on behind me."

Tristan was a little surprised by Sam's quick reaction. Usually, it did end up being him, Sam, and Hugh together on things. But he felt kind of bad because Rosina looked a bit, well, almost put out. And she had seemed so miserable before.

"Come on, you can ride with me," Ryder said. "It'll be better on our shark with just the two of us. We can go faster." He then stared at the other shark and hesitated.

Unlike the others, who'd ridden a shark in the British Virgin Islands, Ryder had never been aboard the shark-mobile. He turned to Tristan. "You're sure about this, shark boy?"

"Yeah," Tristan said from atop the tiger shark. "It's the best."

"Okay, but if I lose any body parts, dude, you're dead."

"Oh, brother," Rosina said, and she surprised them all by grabbing the other shark's fin and swinging her leg up and over it. "Get on behind me," she told Ryder.

Ryder tentatively climbed onto the shark behind Rosina. The shark-and-teen team circled the small skiff once and then headed north. The smaller black-tip sharks and accompanying fish swam at their sides like flanking bodyguards. Ozdale followed cautiously behind on his scooter. Not wanting to attract attention in the more easily seen skiff, Coach Fred and Ms. Sanchez hung back.

The team cruised slowly toward the two-hundred-foot cargo ship. Even at a distance, its gigantic steel hull towered over them. As they got closer, the ship seemed to grow even more colossal. The hull rose up from the water like the towering side of a wide, solid-steel skyscraper. Tristan felt tiny and vulnerable next to the massive ship. He hoped they'd get around it quickly.

The sharks dove to about fifteen feet. Then they turned left and swam along the ship's hull toward its bow. Tristan could hear and feel the thrum of the ship's generators. Ozdale submerged his scooter, following them farther away from the ship. Suddenly, the distinct whine of an outboard engine reverberated through the water. Tristan looked back, thinking it was their skiff.

Boat coming, the tiger shark told Tristan. *It's on the other side of the ship.*

Tristan suggested they go back to the surface and swim around the bow to check it out. The sharks rose up silently. As soon as the teens' heads broke the surface, the sharks leveled off. Tristan whispered to the others, "There's a boat on the other side of the ship."

They were now about thirty feet from the cargo ship's bow. The engine noise got louder, but still they couldn't see the other boat. Sam tried to echolocate and pinpoint its location. "No-go," she whispered. "The ship's in the way."

Nearing the bow, the sharks slowed. Tristan craned his neck, trying to see around the ship's giant front end. He heard a new noise. It was a deep, rumbling sort of mechanical sound. The ship's enormous steel bow then began to swing—toward them. They were about to be squashed like flies on a windshield. Tristan urged his shark-mobile to back up and waved the others behind him away. Unfortunately, their shark-mobiles had very limited back-up capabilities.

Panicking, Tristan swung his arm and knocked Hugh and Sam off the shark. He pushed them as far away from the oncoming wall of steel as possible. Tristan then dove off the shark and kicked as hard as he could. The hull smashed into the lead shark, shoving it sideways. Tristan's heart raced, and the sight of the injured tiger shark made him feel sick, but there was nothing he could do. The bow of the massive ship was still swinging toward them. Tristan quickly decided their best bet was to swim around the ship's bow to the other side. He looked back. Sam and Hugh were close behind him. He waved them on frantically, kicking hard. Tristan glanced farther back, looking for Ryder and Rosina. He was surprised to see that Ozdale had driven his scooter in, grabbed the other two teens, and was now pulling them safely away. The other tiger shark was able to turn in time to escape the oncoming steel monster.

Fortunately, the bow was swinging more slowly

than Tristan thought. Within minutes, he was able to get around it. Sam and Hugh soon joined him. They all treaded water, trying to catch their breath. Adrenaline pulsed through their veins.

"Whoa," Tristan said. "That was close."

"Yeah," Hugh added. "The ship must be leaving or something."

"I don't know about that," Sam said curiously. She pointed to something entering the water about twenty feet from them. They could just make it out. It was the anchor chain. "The anchor's still down."

"That's strange," Tristan noted. Just as he said it, the water around the three teens began to flow. At first, it was like a weak current in a small creek. But then the flow picked up speed. Soon the water was rushing past the campers, pulling and sucking them in like a whirlpool.

"Help!" Sam shouted.

"Grab hold," Tristan said to her and Hugh.

They grabbed hands and together tried to kick against the water's pull. But the current was too strong. Soon all three were tumbling along the surface, surging back toward the giant cargo ship. Tristan felt helpless. He steeled himself, preparing to crash into the ship's hull or get sucked under it. The unconscious tiger shark floated by, also caught in the rushing water.

They rolled and tumbled in the strong flow. Then, abruptly, the water stopped moving, and the teens floated into a calm, eerie darkness. Tristan was relieved to be alive but also confused. What just happened? And where were they?

As he lay low in the water beside Sam and Hugh, Tristan's pulse began to slow. It was pitch black now with no moon. The only thing they could see was the faint glow of their hands and feet. Suddenly, a bright light flared on, nearly blinding the teens. Instinctively, they ducked out of the spotlight's glare and swam into the shadows. Tristan smacked into something big and metal, banging his head. The others rammed into him. Tristan reached out—it felt like a metal wall. Then he heard a boat engine. He squinted into the light's glare. A small powerboat cruised toward them. The teens swam further back into the shadows, hiding their bioluminescent hands and feet.

Minutes later, the water around the teens again began to move—this time in the opposite direction. The current increased. They found a pipe on the metal wall next to them and grabbed hold. Sam, Hugh, and Tristan hung on for dear life as the water again rushed by. Rusty metal cut into their hands. Tristan watched as the lifeless tiger shark was swept away. He noticed the same deep, rumbling mechanical sound as before. Then the water stopped flowing. Tristan let go of the metal pipe and floated silently. He thought he knew where they were but could hardly believe it.

14

IN THE BELLY
OF THE BEAST

OZDALE, ROSINA, AND RYDER RETURNED TO THE skiff to tell Coach Fred and Ms. Sanchez what happened. At least what they *thought* had happened. They weren't exactly sure.

"I saw them swimming toward the bow of the ship," Ozdale said from his scooter. "They should be back soon."

Minutes ticked by and there was no sign of the other campers.

"What exactly did you see again?" Coach asked with concern.

After the others explained again what they saw, Coach Fred turned off the boat's running lights and drove as slowly and as quietly as possible toward the cargo ship. Ozdale followed on his scooter. The ship was at anchor and stationary. Nothing appeared out of the ordinary. They searched for the teens, but there was still no sign of Tristan, Hugh, or Sam. The sharks had disappeared as well.

"Maybe they took off with the sharks?" Rosina whispered hopefully.

"We heard a boat earlier," Ryder added. "Maybe it picked them up."

Coach stared suspiciously at the cargo ship. "Something is off about this ship. Notice how dark it is and that it's anchored with its stern toward shore. All the other ships here are anchored the other way, with their bow toward shore. I have a bad feeling about this. And I don't think our young campers have taken off or were picked up. They'd be back by now. Let's take another look at this ship."

Staying in the shadows, Tristan held up his faintly bioluminescent hands to see Sam and Hugh. The cuts on his hands were healing, but his head still ached from hitting the metal wall. He whispered, "Unbelievable."

"What? Where are we?" Hugh questioned.

"I think we're inside the bow of that cargo ship," he said softly. "It must have opened up and sucked us in."

Hugh's eyes nearly bulged out of his head.

"What's that story?" Sam said. "You know, the one about a guy being swallowed by a whale?"

"I know just how he felt," Hugh groaned.

"Something's not right here," Tristan told them.

"Yeah, like us getting sucked into a giant ship at night," Hugh replied.

The teens looked over to the small boat that had earlier cruised toward them. It had been driven onto a ramp and secured. Two men were now passing several large coolers and tubs from the boat to a few more men on an adjacent platform. A woman dressed in camouflage barked orders at them. After the boat was unloaded and the two men inside had climbed out, the entire group walked into the shadows and disappeared. The spotlight went off and all was dark.

"Wonder what was in those coolers?" Tristan said.

"I bet it has something to do with all the weird stuff going on around here." Sam replied.

Tristan nodded. "C'mon, let's do a little Sea Camp investigating."

Tristan tried to sound confident, but the people on the ship didn't exactly seem like the welcoming type. Still, he had a feeling they were close to discovering what had happened to the missing rays from Stingray City—and all the other animals that had strangely disappeared in Grand Cayman.

Hugh looked at Tristan like he was nuts. "Or maybe we should just find a way out of the belly of the beast before anyone notices we happened to have rolled in."

The water left inside the cargo ship's bow smelled of diesel and rust. Using the faint glow from their hands, Tristan, Sam, and Hugh swam to where the small boat had been secured. Finding a ladder, they climbed up. It led to the platform beside the boat. Hugh was shaky and Sam seemed nervous. Tristan decided he wasn't going to think about what would happen if they were discovered. Besides, he desperately wanted to know what was in the coolers that had been off-loaded from the boat.

The three teens crept quietly along the platform. They found a pile of damp towels at the base of an open metal stairway. Deciding to leave their thin wetsuits on, they dried off with the towels as best they could. Still, as they walked, their feet left a faint watery trail. The stairs led to another platform and an open doorway. The teens went cautiously through into a space about the size of a large closet. It appeared to be a dead end.

Tristan stared at the metal wall in front of them. "I could have sworn those other guys came this way."

"Where else could they have gone?" Sam added, looking around curiously.

The three teens stood and stared at the surrounding metal walls. Tristan couldn't figure it out. Sam put her still faintly glimmering hands out in front and moved closer to the front wall. "Looks like it should open, but there's no doorknob or handle."

"Look around the sides for a switch or lever," Hugh suggested.

Tristan ran his hand along the wall to the left of where they thought a door should be. "Aha. You're brilliant, Hugh." He hit a neatly hidden button. The front wall slid open. "Let's go."

"Or maybe we should just stay here," Hugh countered.

"And do what, wait for those guys to come back

and find us?" Tristan said. "They didn't look like the friendly we-love-guests sort of guys."

"Okay, then let's just look for a way out of here," Hugh urged.

Tristan shrugged. They stepped through the doorway into a wide, dark passageway framed by giant riveted-steel beams. The passageway seemed to run along the ship's hull toward the stern. The teens inched carefully ahead. Tristan stubbed his toe, cursing softly. They rounded a slight curve and saw a light ahead in the distance. It appeared to be coming from an opening into the ship's interior. They crept cautiously toward it.

The campers came to another metal stairway going up. They stopped.

"Which way?" Sam whispered.

"I say we go up and get off this ship," Hugh responded.

Then they heard voices. They were coming from the illuminated area up ahead.

"C'mon," Tristan countered. "Let's just go a little farther to see who's there and what they're up to. Then we can come back, go up, and find a way off this tin can."

Hugh cringed. "I don't know. What if someone comes or they hear us? We should just go up and get off now."

"Don't you want to know what's going on? What they had in those coolers?" Tristan asked.

"Yeah, but I like my life even more. You know, like, more birthdays, more cheeseburgers, that kind of thing."

"We'll make it quick," Tristan said, thinking surely they could sneak just a little bit farther down the passageway to see what was there. Tristan's curiosity and the desire to find the stingrays were overwhelming, stronger than both his fear and common sense.

Tristan put his finger to his lips and crept down the passageway toward the light. Sam followed and Hugh went along reluctantly. The trio moved slowly, staying as quiet as possible. The voices got louder as they approached the light. It was coming from a big square opening to their right. Getting close, the teens flattened themselves against the nearest wall and tucked in behind one of the riveted-steel beams framing the passageway. Tristan nearly tripped, but luckily Sam grabbed his hand and kept him from falling. Tristan whispered, "Thanks." Sam kept hold of his hand, gripping it tightly. Tristan suddenly felt even more awkward than usual. His hand felt all sweaty. He looked down at Sam's hand holding his. She seemed to notice and let go, embarrassed. "Oh, uh, sorry."

Tristan wanted to tell her it was okay. He kind of liked holding her hand, especially then. It somehow made the situation less frightening. But he felt totally tongue-tied. A few incoherent mumbles slipped from his mouth.

"Shh!" Hugh whispered.

As if stuck together with glue, Tristan, Sam, and Hugh leaned past the beam to see what was around the corner.

The skiff made several more passes by the bow and then circled the giant cargo ship. Ozdale followed at a distance on his scooter, keeping an eye out for any sign of the teens. Nothing. Not even a hint of what had happened to Sam, Tristan, and Hugh.

Ms. Sanchez pulled out a cell phone. "I think it's time to call camp and have them isolate their tracker signals. Then I suggest we get in touch with Mr. Hartley. He must know the local authorities. If Tristan, Sam, and Hugh somehow ended up on that ship, maybe we can get them to do a search."

Coach shrugged. "My gut tells me they're onboard and that it's not good. A little equipment, maybe some blasting, and I could get aboard that ship in no time."

"Not the most stealthy or inconspicuous of approaches, Coach," Ms. Sanchez said, shaking her head. "Let's go back and try to get in touch with the authorities through Mr. Hartley. Besides, those kids are smart. Unless they were forcefully taken aboard, the campers will know to stay out of sight and try to find a way off."

"What if they can't?" Rosina said nervously. "What if they're hurt or something?"

Coach pushed the throttle forward, and the skiff sped toward Ozdale's yacht. "I just hope they don't do anything stupid."

Though Tristan didn't have any idea what to expect, he was still surprised by what he saw. It was an enormous compartment, some sort of secret holding area within the bowels of the cargo vessel. A maze of metal catwalks spanned across the hold. The ceiling above the catwalks appeared solid, while below were a series of large tanks. Tristan couldn't see what was inside the tanks, though he could hear water sloshing. Two rough-looking men in dirty gray jumpsuits stood over one of the tanks. One man had a pole with a string attached. He was dangling it down into the tank.

"Here, little fishy," the man taunted. "C'mon, get it." He pulled up on the pole, laughing.

"You can jump higher than that," said the other man to something below. "*Her majesty* said to keep you healthy. If you want the yummy bloody chicken, you'll have to do better."

The two men cackled some more.

"I'll finish feeding the sharks," one said to the other. "Go get something for dinner from the tank in the corner. You know, the one with the lobsters in it. They'll never miss one or two."

"What if you-know-who finds out?"

"I'm not going to tell her. Are you?"

"No, but man, that witch has eyes everywhere. I'm not going to risk it. Remember what happened to Saul? He couldn't wear a shirt for weeks."

Tristan crept further out into the light, trying to see better. Sam grabbed hold of him and yanked him back. "They'll see you," she whispered. "Let's just wait and see if they go away."

"Or we could go back to those stairs and look for a way out of here," Hugh urged again.

"We're this far," Tristan whispered back. "We don't even know if those stairs lead off the ship. And I bet one of those tanks has the stingrays in it. Let's just wait and see if they leave."

The three teens moved back behind the big steel beam in the passageway. They sat down on the metal deck with their backs against the wall, listening to the two men. Sitting in the dark, exhausted, the teens' eyelids soon began to droop.

15

THE HIDDEN HOLD

Tristan woke with a start. It was dark and Sam was shaking him, holding a hand over his mouth. Tristan quickly remembered where he was and nodded. The two of them then gently nudged Hugh to wake him. Tristan wondered how long they'd been out. He couldn't believe they'd fallen asleep—definitely not good mission protocol.

The teens stayed still and listened. All was silent except for the ship's muted thrum and some periodic splashing noises. They got up and crept around the steel beam they'd been hiding behind. The lights were still on in the huge compartment. They leaned across the edge of the opening to peer in. The maze of catwalks was empty.

"C'mon," Tristan said. "Let's see what's in those tanks."

"What if those guys come back?" Hugh said. "We're lucky no one found us. Can't *believe* we fell asleep." The others nodded. "Let's go back, find a way off the ship, and then report this to the others."

"Just a quick peek," Tristan urged. "Then we'll find a way off. Besides, if we don't look in the tanks, we won't know what *exactly* to report."

Then they heard a much louder splash coming from one of the tanks. Tristan had to know what it was. Without waiting for Sam and Hugh to agree, he entered the compartment and jogged across the metal catwalks until he was looking down into one of the largest tanks in the hold. It was at least twenty feet long by ten feet wide. Sam followed. Hugh shook his head and groaned before running to catch up.

Tristan stared into the tank below. The water was crowded with rays. Stingrays and a few spotted eagle rays swam in tight circles, bumping into each other and the sides of the tank. Some of the rays already looked beat up from hitting the walls. Tristan's heart sank. He felt sick. It was a terrible sight. And he knew the rays were panicky and miserable. One of the spotted eagle rays jumped up, seemed to stare at the teens, and then landed with another massive splash.

"Whoa!" said Hugh.

"Whoa is right!" Tristan added. "Guess we know where the missing rays are. This is awful."

Sam crossed over to another tank. "Yeah, and that's not all. There's a whole bunch of fish over here and a couple of sea turtles."

The three teens ran across the network of catwalks,

looking into each of the tanks below. Along with the rays, sea turtles, and fish, they found an octopus, some orange sea stars, a bunch of spiny lobsters, and a tank crowded with sharks. They also discovered several cages along a wall that held two blue iguanas and a red-footed booby.

"I don't think they're fishing for food," Sam said ominously. "Remember what Pete said in Monterey last summer? I bet they're collecting—illegally."

"Yeah," Hugh agreed. "But why? What are they going to do with all these animals?"

"They're probably taking them to a park or aquarium somewhere," Sam added.

"Yeah, and it's probably someplace where it doesn't matter how the animals are collected or treated," Tristan said in disgust. "Remember what Pete told us, about the dolphins in the small pool with dirty water?"

"We have to free them," Sam urged.

"How?" Hugh said.

The teens searched frantically for some way to free the trapped marine life. They forgot about everything and everyone else. All they wanted to do was help the animals. A few minutes later, Tristan stood frustrated and angry over the tank of rays. He hadn't found or thought of any way to help the rays or the other animals trapped in the hidden compartment. Sam was still investigating some pipes that went from the tanks to the ship's hull. But they were small, too tight a fit for even the smallest creatures in the tanks. Hugh headed toward Tristan, shaking his head. He was on the catwalk just passing over the shark tank. "Can't see how we can free them right now. Let's get off the ship and get help."

Tristan nodded. "But first, maybe I should go down there and tell the rays we're not abandoning them."

Suddenly, a loud, body-rattling boom echoed across the hold. The teens froze.

"Hold it right there!" shouted a stocky woman outfitted in a camouflage T-shirt and cargo pants. She had a square jaw, dark buzz-cut hair, and a thin mouth set in a scowl. The woman wasn't tall, but she had a striking presence that demanded respect, if not pee-inducing fear. She also carried a nasty-looking whip curled at her hip that added to the I-could-kill-you-at-any-moment look. At her sides, and in front of the metal door they'd just slammed open, were two frighteningly large men. They wore gray, dirt-stained shirts and cargo pants with weapons slung over their backs.

Tristan swiveled around, looking for a quick escape route. He ran for the passageway they'd entered through. Two more men appeared at the end of the catwalk, blocking his path.

"I don't know who you are or where you came from," barked the woman. "But I don't take kindly to stowaways or uninvited guests. Men, round up our young friends, here."

Having nowhere else to go, Tristan ran back and jumped in with the rays. Sam backed away from the men on the catwalk, and Hugh, seeing what Tristan had done, jumped into the tank below.

The rays swarmed around Tristan. He quickly explained to them who he was, why he was there, and that things hadn't gone exactly as he hoped. Sam tried to make a run for it, but the thugs grabbed her.

"Captain, sir—I mean, ma'am," said one of the men blocking the passageway exit. He was a scrawny and particularly unkempt member of the crew, resembling a truly scary scarecrow. "One of 'em jumped in with the rays. The other's in with them sharks."

"I can see that, Iggy. And how many times do I have to tell you? Don't call me ma'am. I'm not your old, doting granny," shouted the captain. "Well, don't just stand there; go get them."

One of the heavily muscled men started to climb down the ladder into the ray tank. His bulging arms were covered with tattoos of pirate-related paraphernalia: knives, an anchor, and ships, along with a skull and crossbones. The scrawny guy ran to the tank with the sharks. "Hey, there's no one in here. Where'd he go?"

"You idiot!" the captain yelled. "I saw the kid jump in. He's in there."

Scarecrow Man looked into the tank and then turned back to the captain. "No, ma'am—I mean, *sir*. I mean, *Captain*. Just a wetsuit and some shorts floating on the surface. Maybe the sharks ate 'em."

"Any blood?" asked another of the crew.

Iggy looked back into the tank. "No."

"Then how'd they eat 'em?"

He turned again to the captain. "One big gulp?"

The captain squinted and glared at the man like he just said that little green men from Mars had whisked the boy away to their spaceship.

Overhearing the exchange, Sam smiled. Tristan,

however, hadn't heard about Hugh's disappearing act in the shark tank; he was too busy trying to avoid the big, ugly guy who had climbed down into the ray tank. The man's nose was hooked and crooked. Spittle flew out of his wide, cracked lips. But the worst thing was his teeth, which were ragged and brown and dripping with slimy globs of drool. Tristan looked away. Luckily, the rays were helping him. They kept getting in the giant man's way and jumping onto his back as he tried to grab hold of Tristan. Two men watching from above started laughing. "Having a hard time down there, Tiny? One teenager in a small tank too much for you?"

The man let out a roar similar to what Tristan imagined an angry grizzly bear sounded like. With three giant stingrays clinging to his back, the man bounded across the tank. Tristan backed up as far as possible. The man reached for him with an arm as wide around as Tristan's thighs. With nowhere else to go, Tristan took a breath, dove under the guy's legs, and swam to the other side of the tank. Unfortunately, above him, the two other men were waiting. They dropped a heavy net on top of him. Tristan struggled to escape. He understood exactly how the rays in the tank felt — closed in, trapped, and panicked. Meanwhile, one of the rays jabbed the man in the tank with the barb on its tail. The big man cursed. "I'll kill 'em. Kill 'em all with my bare hands!"

Tristan stopped struggling and willed himself to calm down, thinking about the rays. *Stop!* he silently told them. *Get away. He'll kill you. It'll be okay. We'll find a way out. And then we'll come back for you.*

Tristan said it to calm the stingrays, but he wasn't sure he believed it. Why hadn't he listened to Hugh? They should have tried to find a way off the ship first thing. Now they were in serious trouble, and it was all his fault.

Caught up in the net, Tristan was hauled out of the tank. He swore at the men and himself for getting into such a mess. He'd been so confident—*too* confident— that they could just take a peek into the tanks and then find a way off the ship. Tristan looked at his feet. With the new pills, the effects lasted much longer, and his webbing had returned. He hoped the captain and her men wouldn't notice. He tried to hide his webs as best he could, hoping they would disappear quickly.

The captain and crew's attention, however, was now focused back on the shark tank and the scrawny guy hovering over it. "No teenager, ma'am. I swear."

The captain glared at Iggy.

"I mean *sir*. *Poof*, he's gone."

"I'll make you go *poof*, Iggy," the captain responded. "Get your skinny butt down there and take a closer look. Or do I need to come over there myself?"

"No . . . no, Captain. But you want me to go in there with the sharks?"

"Tiny," said the captain to the hulk of a man climbing out of the ray tank. "Could you go over and help little old Iggy out? Before I cut him up and use him as chum."

Tiny yanked the stingray barb from his thigh and grinned, or grimaced, it was hard to tell which. "Sure thing, Captain."

Hugh stealthily popped up for a breath and then hunkered back down against the bottom of the tank. After jumping in, he had swiftly wiggled out of his wetsuit and shorts, all the while trying to stay as far away from the sharks as possible. He then pressed his body flat against the floor of the tank. Using his talent for camouflage, he mimicked the tank's color and texture. It was the trick he had perfected last summer. Every time Iggy turned his back on the tank to talk to the captain, Hugh popped up for air and then went back down. But he was getting tired, and his concentration was fading. It didn't help that he was in a tank filled with sharks, and who knew how hungry they were.

Iggy and the big man, Tiny, looked again into the tank. Hugh was on the bottom, mimicking its color and texture, while several of the sharks swam in tight circles directly above him.

Tiny stared in astonishment. Iggy shrugged and held up his hands. "See what I mean? No kid."

Tiny waddled down the ladder into the tank. He reached out to grab the wetsuit floating on the surface. One of the sharks lunged for his hand, its razor-sharp teeth gnashing nastily. The man snatched the wetsuit and scrambled up the ladder. "Captain, for once, Iggy's right. No sign of the kid." He held up the wetsuit and looked at his hand. "Or blood."

"He must have climbed out without us seeing," Iggy said, scanning the area around the tank.

"You think?" the captain shouted. "You skinny imbecile. Why do I keep you around?"

"Because I'm good with electronics?" Iggy answered very seriously.

"Lucky for that," the captain snapped. "Stay here and find him. He's got to be around here somewhere. Don't come back until you have him in your scrawny little hands."

"Yes, ma'am."

The captain stalked away, muttering murderous curses.

Having been removed from the net, Tristan was led away beside Sam. They were marched behind the captain, surrounded by the armed crew. Tristan hung his head. He also wanted to plug his nose. The men around him stunk. The combined smell of diesel and seriously bad body odor was enough to nearly knock him out. Sam made a face at him and pinched her nose.

"Bring 'em along, boys," said the captain. "Into the brig for now."

16

CAT AND MOUSE

HUGH PULLED ON HIS SWIM TRUNKS, WHICH TINY had fortunately left behind. While he was thanking the sharks, even though they wouldn't understand him, Hugh heard a voice in his head: *No problem, matey. We were happy to help.*

Hugh looked around, confused. He'd never been able to talk to sharks before.

Over here! On the blacktip with the big schnoz.

A blacktip shark with a particularly long snout twisted its head back and stared menacingly. But it wasn't looking at Hugh. The shark was eyeing a small gray fish attached to its body.

No offense, said the remora to the shark.

The remora detached itself from the shark and swam to Hugh. Two black stripes ran the length of its narrow, four-inch-long, gray body, and it had a very peculiar head. The fish's head was flat and topped by an oval-shaped, ribbed suction cup. The remora tried to attach its bizarre suction-cup head to Hugh, who in turn pushed it away. After several minutes of back and forth, Hugh gave up and let the fish suck onto his stomach. The remora told Hugh how unlucky it was, having been on a shark that was captured. Hugh then silently said he had to leave, and asked the small fish to thank the sharks for their help and for not eating him.

Iggy, who was still searching the hold for Hugh, yelled out, "Come out, come out, wherever you are! I know you're still in here, kid."

Hugh crept quietly up the shark tank's ladder. He trembled from head to toe. He raised his head just above the lip of the tank, searching for the man. Iggy was at the base of the tanks on nearly the opposite side of the hold.

Hugh took a deep breath and climbed onto the open catwalk above the tank. Staying low, he crawled nervously across the metal grating. The catwalk shuddered and creaked. Hugh froze.

"We're not going to hurt you," said Iggy, overly sweetly. "We just want to know who you are. Besides, mommy and daddy must be missing little wiggums."

Hugh rolled his eyes and continued crawling. He headed for the opening they'd come in through. At the edge of the passageway, he paused and took another deep breath. Hugh then stood up, ready to run.

"There you are, you little rat!"

Hugh ran, jumped over a beam, and sprinted down
the metal deck of the wide passageway.

Tristan and Sam were thrown unceremoniously into
the ship's brig, a small cabin one level below and
behind the ship's bridge. Along the way, Tristan had
counted six flights of stairs as they'd been marched up
from the lower deck. Without a word, the door was
locked and they were left alone. The two teens sat on
the bottom bed of the bunk in the cabin.

"Look on the bright side," Tristan said, noting his
now normal hands and feet. "They didn't notice my
webbing. And I bet Coach Fred is planning to storm
the ship or something. They have to know we're here."

"Yeah," Sam agreed, twirling the tracking bracelet
that each camper wore on missions. "Back at camp
they'll know for sure. And Ryder or Rosina must have
seen us get sucked into the ship. *I think.*"

Just then they heard a thunderous rumble, and the
floor began to vibrate.

"Uh-oh," Sam said.

"What?" Tristan asked. "What's that noise?"

"The engines."

A loud rattling echoed throughout the ship as one
of its massive anchor chains was pulled up off the seafloor.

"This is *not* good," Tristan groaned.

Hugh ran as if his life depended on it, since it probably did. He sprinted down the passageway to the metal stairway they'd seen earlier. He dashed up as fast as he could. Iggy was behind him. "You can't escape, rat! I'm coming for ya."

Hugh swung around and sprinted up another flight of stairs. At the top, he paused, breathing hard. He'd never been very athletic, more of a tech geek kind of kid. Hugh looked around at his options—or lack thereof. Then he heard pounding on the stairs below. "I *see* you!"

Hugh scrambled up another flight of stairs and then down another wide and long metal passageway. He knocked over a big stack of coolers so they littered the floor like an obstacle course. At the next stairway, Hugh raced up. The stairs led to the ship's open deck. He ran out into the gray, early-morning light. To Hugh's left sat a stack of giant orange, rectangular metal containers. To his right was the ship's rail, and past that, just ocean. He leaned over. It was a very long way down; too far to jump.

"I've got you now, rat!" shouted Iggy from the base of the stairs leading to the open deck.

Hugh sprinted into a narrow space between the stacks of containers. He squeezed through and ran along an open alleyway between the containers. Hugh then stopped and tried to open one of the crates— locked.

"No place to hide, kid," Iggy called out as he jogged onto the deck and began searching for the boy.

Hugh slid between two more stacks of containers and came out on the opposite side of the ship. He leaned over the rail—still a very, very long way down. Then something caught his eye—a potential hiding place. Gasping for breath, Hugh climbed in.

"I know you're here, little wiggums," Iggy taunted as he searched the deck. Several minutes later, he approached Hugh's hiding spot. "Just a matter of time before I find you."

The ship's two enormous anchors were now fixed firmly against the hull. On the bridge, the captain ordered all cargo and equipment secured. She notified the port captain they were leaving, spoke with the ship's engineer, and had the navigator put their course into the GPS and electronic chart system. As the sun began to rise, she turned to her helmsman. "Ahead slow. Take us out. We are leaving Grand Cayman *now*."

"Yes, sir."

17

COAST GUARD

It was a morning like any other for most people on Grand Cayman as a large cruise ship headed into port and a slightly smaller cargo ship made its way out. As was the norm around Christmastime, the trade winds blew from the east. The water off George Town was smooth and calm. The sun rose higher in the sky, and the puffy white clouds lining the coast turned conch-shell pink.

Inside the small cabin aboard the cargo ship, Tristan paced while Sam sat on the bunk, tapping her fingers nervously. Tristan was frustrated, angry, and scared. They were trapped, and the captain definitely was not taking them out for a pleasure cruise. This time he'd screwed up royally.

"Hugh's still out there," Sam said, smiling weakly. "He'll get help."

Tristan just nodded. He hoped she was right, but doubted it. How was Hugh going to get off the ship and not get caught?

"Have some faith," Sam said. "Hugh's supersmart and a great mimic; he'll find a way off. And remember, Coach Fred and the others *must* know we're aboard."

Even though he knew it was locked, Tristan went to the door and tried the knob. "I should have listened to Hugh earlier. We should have looked for a way off the ship first thing. I'm such an idiot."

"Then so am I," Sam said. "I wanted to see what was in those tanks too."

"You're just saying that to be nice," Tristan responded. "This is all my fault."

"Hugh will think of something. I know it."

Tristan knew Sam was trying to make him feel better. And he liked her all the more for it. But he couldn't get past the fact that his cocky overconfidence had put the lives of his two best friends at risk, as well as his own. Not to mention all the sea creatures stuck in the tanks they wouldn't be able to save.

The noise of the vessel's engines increased, and the vibration became steadier.

"We're speeding up," Sam said.

Tristan dropped miserably onto the bunk next to Sam. His head sank into his hands. Sam put her arm over his shoulders. Tristan didn't even notice.

Hugh cautiously slid the tarp from over his head and popped up to look around. No Iggy in sight, but wind now whipped his face and hair. The ship was moving. Something then smacked the back of Hugh's head. He instantly ducked back down under the tarp. He was in a small inflatable boat he discovered stored on deck next to the railing. Hugh sat still and silent. Nothing happened. He slowly rose up again to peek out from under the tarp. Again, something struck his head. Hugh swung around. Perched on the rail behind him was a medium-sized bird with gray wings, black legs, and a white neck and chest. Its sharp beak was bright orange. The bird also had a funny tuft of black feathers sticking out from the back of its otherwise white head, making it look like it was having a really bad hair day. The bird eyed him and then pecked at Hugh's hand.

"Ouch," Hugh whispered, waving his hand. "Shoo. Go away."

The bird jumped up, flapped its wings, and flew south, away from the ship.

Hugh leaned over the side of the ship. Far below, the water rushed by the hull like a raging river. More than ever, jumping was not an option.

On the bridge, Captain Opal Johnson sat rigidly in a raised padded chair. No one on the crew ever dared call her Opal. In fact, no one had called her that since elementary school. After that it was Johnny, Johnson, J-Whip, and now Captain. She stared out through a row of wide windows toward the ship's bow and the ocean ahead. What Captain Johnson lacked in height or strength, she made up for in sheer ruthlessness. On this trip, she'd already thrown one of the crew overboard for trying to skip out on deck-washing duty. Another man was whipped after he told a joke about women being unlucky aboard ships. She jumped from the chair, pulled a cell phone from her pocket, and walked to the far left side of the bridge, out of earshot of the crew.

The captain punched in a number. It was answered on the first ring. "Sir, it's me. We've had a minor complication and are leaving a few days early. We didn't get everything we'd hoped. One dolphin got away. But it's an excellent haul." From the expression on her face, it was clear that whomever she was talking to was not pleased with the news.

"Yes, sir, we should have plenty of opportunity along the way to pick up additional cargo or replacements for those that don't make it. We typically lose a few along the way."

The captain listened in silence for a minute, scowling.

"No, sir. No need to send any more *men*. I've got this covered. Have I ever let you down? And our little problems will disappear once we hit the open ocean."

The captain disconnected and shoved the phone back into her pocket. "I want no more surprises," she bellowed to no one in particular. "I'm going to my cabin. Let me know when we're far enough out to legally dump our waste and the other island trash we seem to have picked up." She snickered at her joke. The crew members on the bridge all laughed loudly. She glared at them. The men were immediately silent and ducked their heads as if deeply concentrating on whatever they were supposed to be doing.

Just as she was leaving the bridge, the buzz of the ship's phone stopped her. She turned to the helmsman as he picked it up. "Bridge." The man paused, listening. "Are you sure? Okay, got it. Captain's not going to like it."

Captain Johnson stared at the man.

"Captain, there's a Cayman Coast Guard vessel approaching off our stern."

"Didn't you see it on the radar?"

The man shrugged in response. The captain gave him a fiery look as she grabbed a set of binoculars and stalked to the windows looking aft. A vessel with flashing blue lights was approaching.

The ship's radio crackled. "Cargo ship *Dawn Oasis*, stop your engines and prepare to be boarded. This is the Cayman Coast Guard!"

The captain picked up the ship's phone and rapidly punched in a number. She spoke quickly and severely. "Take our guests back to the hidden hold and secure them. Make sure they won't be making any noise. Now!"

She turned to Iggy, who was slumped in one corner of the bridge. "You're sure that other kid went overboard?"

"Pretty sure, ma—sir."

"You'd better be right, or tonight you'll be sleeping with the fishes."

Iggy scampered to the door leading off the bridge. "Maybe I'll just go take another look around."

The captain glared menacingly and picked up the microphone for the ship's radio. She paused.

"Cargo ship *Dawn Oasis*, stop your engines and prepare to be boarded. Stand down. This is the Cayman Coast Guard!"

With a sigh of annoyance, Captain Johnson pressed the transmit button. "This is Captain Johnson of the *Dawn Oasis*. We are stopping our engines and standing down. We'll be ready to receive your boarding party to the port."

She nodded to the helmsman, who then throttled down. The ship's engines quieted and the huge vessel began to slow.

18

TIED UP

THE LOUD ROAR OF THE ENGINES QUIETED. TRIStan felt the ship's motion change. Sam must have noticed as well. They both got up from the bunk. Tristan put his ear against the door. "I wonder what's going on."

"Ship's definitely slowing," Sam noted.

"Yeah, but why?"

Tristan heard footsteps approaching and stepped back from the door. It swung open. The tattooed giant of a man, Tiny, stood there with something akin to a grin on his butt-ugly face. Tristan tried not to look at the man's rotting, brown teeth. Behind him were two more of the smelly crew. "C'mon, kids, time for a little stroll on deck."

Tristan didn't like the sound of that. Was "stroll on

deck" another way of saying you're about to be thrown off the ship to a very horrible and painful death? But why would the ship slow down for that? He assumed it would be faster and more painful if the ship were going full speed. In lieu of a better—or *any*—choice, Tristan and Sam left the cabin and followed the hefty, and still very stinky, brute of a man.

"Where are you taking us?" Tristan blurted out, while trying not to breathe through his nose. "What are you going to do with us?"

"Questions, questions," Tiny growled. "Who said you could talk?" He smacked Tristan on the head.

Tristan squeezed his lips tight, trying to squelch his tendency to blurt things out or make sarcastic comments. He didn't want to make their situation any worse than it already was. Then again, could it get any worse? Not only were he and Sam probably about to die, but even worse, it was his fault. Fear mixed with tremendous guilt felt like a giant weight on Tristan's shoulders. Then anger flared within him. Tristan was angry about their situation, about it being his fault, and furious about the trapped sea creatures. It was like a bolt of lightning jolting him out of hopelessness. Tristan needed to channel his emotions and be strong, like Director Davis had told them to do in the British Virgin Islands. As they walked, Tristan pushed the guilt and the fear aside and tried to make a mental map of the ship. He'd look for an opportunity to do something, anything, to keep them alive and get them off the ship. He had to.

Tiny led them down stairs, across an open deck to about midship, and down some more stairs. Inside the ship it was dim, but now that it was light outside, Tristan could see that almost everything around him was painted bright red. The ship was, in essence, a colossal maze of red steel beams, decks, stairs, walls, and wide passageways. Several sets of stairs later, the group ran into Iggy. He was out of breath and even more disheveled than before.

"What's got you so buggered up?" Tiny asked.

"You haven't seen that other kid, have you?" Iggy asked worriedly.

Tiny shook his head. Iggy scampered away as Tristan and Sam exchanged a hopeful glance.

They eventually stopped in front of a red steel wall. The area seemed familiar to Tristan, but then again, most of the ship looked pretty much the same. Tiny stepped to the side and hit a button hidden behind a steel beam. The wall slid open, revealing a large, hidden compartment. It was the hold with the tanks in it.

"Looks like these are your new quarters," Tiny cackled. "And I know just where to put you two."

"Oh, that's okay," Tristan said. "We're fine out here, *strolling the deck.*"

"Funny, kid," Tiny muttered.

Tristan was serious. Tiny pushed him and Sam roughly across several catwalks to a holding tank in the corner.

"After you," Tiny ordered, nodding to a ladder that went down into the tank.

Sam began climbing down. Tristan followed, thinking, *At least there isn't any water in the tank.* It was empty and dry. Once they were at the base, Tiny climbed down to join them. He took two thick plastic zip ties from his pocket. "Ladies first."

Tiny then began to secure Sam's wrists to the ladder.

"Ouch! Hey, watch it," Sam snarled and tried to kick the man's shins. But for such a big guy, he moved quickly out of the way and then pulled the zip tie snug.

"Your turn," Tiny said as he grabbed Tristan's wrists and lashed him to the other side of the ladder.

He turned to the crew above, watching. "You guys have anything we can use as gags?"

One man tugged at a gray sock streaked with grease and numerous other unidentifiable substances.

Please, no, Tristan prayed.

"Captain said not to kill 'em just yet," Tiny chortled at the man. "Grab some of the netting. That'll do the trick."

One of the men pulled a frighteningly big knife from a sheath on a line around his waist. He then used it to cut two pieces of netting from a pile.

"Look, no need for that," Sam said pitifully. "Who's gonna hear us in here? Besides, we're just kids." She tried the pretend-crying thing, sobbing, "You should just let us go. We won't tell anyone. I mean, who cares about some lousy sea creatures anyway?"

"Good try, kid. But I gotta follow the captain's orders. You do not want to cross the queen of mean."

With his smelly hands, Tiny shoved the netting into their mouths and tied it off around the back of their

heads. Tristan gagged. The smell of old fish, in addition to the man's reek of diesel and body odor, pushed
the stench meter past repulsive. Sam appeared ready
to pass out.

"Okay, now. You all have a nice stay, and we'll see
you in a little while. When the pool opens." Chuckling,
Tiny climbed the ladder and left the two teens tied up
and gagged inside the holding tank. Tristan couldn't
see them, but he heard the other two men snickering
as they walked across the catwalks and then closed the
sliding steel wall behind them. He and Sam struggled
to spit out the gags and slip their hands from the plastic
ties. Both were too tight. Soon their wrists were red
and raw, and their gags no looser than before. The two
teens slumped onto the floor of the holding tank.

The commander aboard the Cayman Coast Guard
vessel waited until the cargo ship's forward momen-
tum had all but ceased. He brought the patrol boat up
alongside the *Dawn Oasis* at an open cargo hatchway
about midship on the port side. A rope ladder was lowered, and a party of five climbed aboard the cargo ship.
The group consisted of the Coast Guard commander,
two heavily armed lieutenants, Coach Fred, and Ms.
Sanchez.

"Welcome aboard the *Dawn Oasis*," said Captain
Johnson in a tone the crew had never heard her use:
nice. She was now wearing a clean, white, and well-

pressed uniform with black epaulets at the shoulders, each with four gold stripes. "What can I do for you gentlemen? Is there some sort of problem?"

The Coast Guard commander nodded respectfully to the cargo ship's captain. "No problem, Captain. Just a routine random inspection before you leave Cayman waters."

"I see," said Captain Johnson, warily eyeing the non–Coast Guard members of the party. "If you'll follow me, I'll take you to the bridge and show you my paperwork. Everything should be in order. We have nothing to hide."

One of the stinky thugs stood nearby. He was dressed as cleanly and as neatly as possible. He snickered at the captain's words. She flashed him a warning look that would wither a giant redwood.

"Thank you, Captain," the Coast Guard officer responded. "While we go to the bridge, my associates here and one of my men would like to examine the rest of the ship."

"Of course. A couple of my crew will accompany them. My ship is like an open book. Go wherever you'd like—though I hope this won't take long. I have a schedule to keep."

Coach Fred and Ms. Sanchez exchanged a momentary glance of suspicion. As the group left for the bridge, Coach Fred whispered something to the Coast Guard lieutenant who would be accompanying him and Ms. Sanchez.

"We'd like to take a look at the bow first," the lieutenant said to the cargo ship's first officer. The man

nodded and led the way. Two of Captain Johnson's
beefy crew trailed behind.

Back in the tank, tied to the ladder, and trapped in the
hidden hold, Tristan once again steeled himself. He
was determined not to give up or give in to fear. He
kicked the side of the tank to see how loud a noise
he could make. It was little more than a muffled thud.
He scanned the empty tank, looking for anything that
might be helpful. Nothing. Then Tristan thought he
heard something. He looked at Sam. She nodded, indicating she'd heard it too. It sounded like the steel wall
sliding open.

Tristan and Sam stood and stretched up as far as
possible, trying to see if someone had entered the
compartment. But tied to the ladder, they couldn't
see past the lip of the tank. Tristan wondered if Tiny
and his goons were back already, getting ready to send
them on one last swim. They heard the door close
again. Then silence.

A few moments later, the teens heard faint creaking
noises. It sounded like someone or something was on
the catwalks above the tanks. Tristan looked questioningly at Sam, who shrugged in response. They tried
again but still couldn't see past the top of the tank.
Tristan listened to the soft creaking of the metal catwalks. Someone was definitely up there.

"Well, that doesn't look very comfortable," Hugh

said, standing over the tank in his swim trunks, grinning.

Tristan tried to laugh, shout, or just thank Hugh for finding them, but with the gag in, it all came out as one big muffled groan. Hugh scrambled down the ladder and undid Sam's gag.

"Man, are we glad to see you," Sam said.

Hugh then untied Tristan's gag.

"Yeah, Hugh. How'd you get away and find us?"

"To make a long story short," Hugh told them. "I hid in a boat on deck. Then, when I was climbing out, I saw that scrawny guy again and decided to follow him, kinda hoping I'd find you guys or a way off the ship. While I was following him, he ran into that big guy leading you down here. So I just trailed behind and then hid until they were gone."

Tristan was impressed and utterly grateful. He looked at the heavy plastic ties securing his wrists to the ladder. "Do you still have your tool with the knife in it?"

Hugh shook his head. "Sorry, left it back at Sunset House."

"Look around for something to cut these things off with," Sam suggested hurriedly.

"Hey, I've got an idea," Tristan said. "Remember the stingray barb that was stuck in our friend Tiny's leg?

"Gotcha," Hugh responded. "I'll be back in a minute. Oh, and by the way, I know how they found us before. There's a security camera in here. I heard them say that it's turned off right now because of some sort of inspection."

"Inspection?" Tristan questioned.

"I bet it's Coach Fred and Ms. Sanchez!" Sam said. "Hurry! Let's get out of here and find them."

Hugh scrambled up the ladder and searched the catwalks.

"Try the floor next to the stingray tank," Tristan shouted.

"Nothing there," Hugh yelled back. "Hold on, there's something at the bottom *inside* the stingray tank. I think that might be it."

"Climb down. They won't hurt you," Tristan yelled. He looked at Sam with an expression that said, *At least, I don't think they will.*

"Uh, okay. Hold on, I'm going in." Hugh climbed tentatively down the ladder into the tank. "Nice rays. I'm here to help."

Tristan smiled. "C'mon, Hugh, hurry it up before the inspection ends or someone comes, like that stinkman Tiny."

"Or before they turn the camera back on," Sam added.

Tristan looked around for the camera. But he still couldn't see much from where he was in the tank. He heard a quick splash, some sloshing noises, and then, "I got it!"

Dripping wet, Hugh ran over and climbed back down into the holding tank. He held up the serrated stingray barb and then used it to slice through the plastic zip ties, first releasing Sam and then Tristan.

"Glad Tiny didn't keep that as a souvenir," Sam said.

"No joke," Tristan added as he climbed out of the tank. He headed for the nearest exit. "Let's get out of here!"

The closest way out of the compartment was through the metal door that the captain and crew had come through earlier. It took all three of the teens to unlatch it and swing the heavy door open. On the other side was another solid steel wall. Tristan saw a button to the side and pressed it. The fake wall slid open. They were staring down a narrow and dimly lit hallway with a series of doors along the sides. They crept slowly to one of the doors. It was open a crack. Silently, Sam pushed it open just enough to see inside. It was a crew cabin with a bunk bed, simple desk, chair, and closet. Then they heard voices. "They'll never find a thing. That hold's hidden by the fake compartment above it, and there's no trace of those kids anywhere else on the ship." It sounded like some of the crew farther down the hallway, and they were headed toward the teens.

Tristan, Hugh, and Sam looked around for a place to hide. They considered going into the crew cabin, but what if that's where the men were going? With no other choice, they sprinted back the way they'd come. They opened the fake wall and slipped quietly back into the hidden hold. Tristan prayed the men hadn't seen them or the wall closing. They raced along the catwalks to the other exit, the sliding steel wall that opened into one of the ship's wide passageways along the hull.

Tristan hit the button to open the sliding wall.

"We've got to get out and find them before the inspection ends. I counted. We're four flights down and in about the middle of the ship, I think."

"C'mon," Hugh said, taking off down the passageway. He stopped at the first set of stairs. "This way."

At the next deck up, the teens paused. Cautiously, they leaned out of the stairwell to check the passageway for any of the crew or the inspection team. No one was there. They raced up another flight of stairs and checked the next deck—still no one.

"Let's go up to the open deck," Hugh whispered. "Maybe we'll be able to see them from there."

Or be seen by the queen of mean and her smelly thugs, Tristan thought as he followed Hugh.

The tour of the bow had proven disappointingly normal. The Coast Guard lieutenant, Ms. Sanchez, and Coach Fred were also shown the forwardmost cargo hold. It was empty, having been unloaded in Grand Cayman. They were then led around the deck above the bow and shown the ship's double hull, giant anchors, and anchor windlass. When Coach Fred asked about the inside of the bow itself, the crew said it was a holding tank for ballast water when needed. There was no evidence of anything unusual. The group then headed around the containers remaining on deck and was shown two giant cargo holds now locked and ready for transport. When Ms. Sanchez asked what was inside, the crew led them up to the bridge to see images from the security cameras onboard, including those in the cargo holds. Again, there was nothing unusual or suspicious.

On the bridge, the Coast Guard commander had just finished going over the ship's paperwork with Captain Johnson. He looked at Coach Fred and Ms. Sanchez and shook his head before saying, "Thank you, Captain. Everything seems to be in order. We'll let you be on your way."

"Thank *you*," said Captain Johnson.

As the group was exiting the bridge, the Coast Guard commander turned back to the ship's captain. "Oh, and you haven't seen a couple of teenagers running around out here, have you?"

The captain laughed. It was an odd sound, as if she wasn't quite sure how to do it. "Out here? Ha. What would some teenagers be doing out here? Of course not, Commander; I run a very tight ship."

The Coast Guard commander nodded to the captain and led the others back to their boat. After climbing aboard, Coach Fred turned to the man. "The tracking signals say they're onboard this ship. We need to do a more thorough search."

"Are you sure the technology is working? Maybe it's a software glitch and those kids are off swimming somewhere or partying it up onshore. I've got a teenager of my own at home."

"Believe me," Ms. Sanchez said. "These kids are not off partying somewhere. They are well trained."

"Trained? Teenagers? I can barely get mine to make his bed or clean up his room. Look, without solid evidence, I can't do anything more. We have laws here."

"Yeah, well, sometimes laws need to be broken," Coach urged.

"Not today and not on my watch," the commander said as he steered the boat away from the cargo ship, toward shore. "Come up with some solid evidence and I'll stop that ship before it enters international waters. But for now, there's nothing more I can do."

19

VOLUNTEERS FOR DOOM

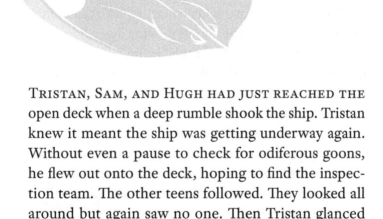

Tristan, Sam, and Hugh had just reached the open deck when a deep rumble shook the ship. Tristan knew it meant the ship was getting underway again. Without even a pause to check for odiferous goons, he flew out onto the deck, hoping to find the inspection team. The other teens followed. They looked all around but again saw no one. Then Tristan glanced over the rail toward shore. A small white boat was moving past the stern, toward Grand Cayman.

Tristan pointed to the boat. "That must be them. We're too late."

Standing next to him, Sam jumped up and down, waving her arms. "Hey! Over here! We're still here! Come back."

Tristan and Hugh glanced grimly at one another

and then tackled Sam. Tristan put his hand over her mouth as they knocked her to the deck.

"Hey, what was that for?" Sam asked after they released her.

"Sorry," Tristan said. "But it's too late. They're too far away."

"Yeah," Hugh added. "And you were yelling kinda loud."

Pushed by its massive, churning propellers, the cargo ship began to pick up speed, and the three teens scurried back into the stairwell.

"Now what?" Sam asked dejectedly. "We can't jump off, especially since the ship is moving again."

"That's for sure," Hugh said. "If the fall doesn't kill us, we'll be splattered against the hull or chopped up by the propellers."

"Nice, Hugh," Sam said.

"Hey, I'm just sayin'."

"They *must* know we're here," Tristan said, twirling his tracker bracelet. "Maybe they're leaving to come up with a plan or something. You know how Coach Fred is . . . likes his plans."

"Maybe," Hugh muttered.

"Well, I don't know about you, but I, for one, don't want to sit around and wait to see what his plan is," Sam said.

"Yeah, me either," Tristan agreed. "We can't hide forever, and besides, those goons are going to know we escaped."

"Maybe we can find a way to slow this tub down," Sam suggested.

"And let Coach Fred and the others know we're still here and ready to get off," Tristan added.

"How are we going to do either of those things?" Hugh asked.

Tristan shook his head. They needed a plan—quick.

"Hey, Hugh. Did you see any flares while you were running around before, or something else we could use to signal the others?" Sam asked.

"I was kinda busy at the time. Besides, I don't even know what a flare looks like."

"What about the sea creatures?" Tristan offered. "What if we release a couple to bring a message to the others?"

"They'd have to survive the drop," Hugh said. "And avoid being squashed against the hull and chopped up for fish food."

Tristan and Sam glared at Hugh, who just shrugged in response.

"Let's ask them if they could do it," Sam said. "And then try to think of a way to slow down the ship."

They crept cautiously back down to the hidden hold. Tristan stayed on the lookout for the crew, hoping Sam's earlier shouting and hand waving hadn't attracted any attention. As they approached the compartment, he said, "About that security camera. Let's see if we can find it first."

The three teens leaned into the hold and scanned the area, looking for a camera.

"Over there," Hugh said, pointing to a wall to their left. "Can't believe I didn't see it before." He hit himself in the head.

"Is it still off?" Sam asked.

Hugh stared at the camera. "I think so. See, there's a red light right below the lens. I bet it turns green when it's on."

"I hope you're right," Tristan said. "Can we disconnect it or something?"

"I don't even think I can reach it," Hugh answered, walking to a spot directly below the fish-eye camera. It was mounted about twelve feet above the catwalk.

"Let's throw something over it," Tristan suggested. "That could at least buy us some time if they turn it on."

Each of the teens began searching for something to use to cover the camera. Sam found a pile of towels and grabbed one. "How about this?"

They ran back to the camera. Sam jumped up and tried to throw the towel over it. She missed. Being the tallest, Tristan tried next. No luck.

"Let me get on your shoulders," Sam said to Tristan.

Hugh helped her climb from the railing of the catwalk to Tristan's shoulders. He then passed her the towel.

"I think I can reach it," Sam said as she wobbled and stretched her arm up toward the camera. A little bit short and off-balance, she tossed the towel before jumping to the catwalk. It landed right on the camera.

Hugh hugged Sam. "Perfect!"

Tristan was about to hug Sam too, when he stopped short and decided to high-five her instead. "Good job." It was an awkward moment.

"So, uh, which of the animals in here could survive the jump from the ship?" Sam asked.

Tristan immediately thought about the red-footed booby in the cage to the side. But none of them could speak bird to tell it what to do. Hugh just shook his head skeptically.

"Let's ask them," Sam said.

Hugh remained unmoving, looking doubtful. "Yeah, like, which one of you wants to go on a suicide mission?"

"C'mon," Sam urged. "Just give it a try and see what they say."

Hugh walked glumly across the catwalks, muttering something about being mashed, sliced, and diced. Meanwhile, Tristan climbed down into the tank with the rays. Sam stood on lookout above, listening for anyone coming.

The rays instantly swarmed around Tristan.

Yo, you came back for us.

Hey, bobo, I knew you would.

We're saved!

Tristan hated to interrupt the celebration, especially since he didn't exactly have good news. In fact, he was about to ask for volunteers to jump to what might be a swift, ugly, and very painful death. *Uh, hi again.*

So, mon, what's the plan? one of the stingrays asked.

Tristan hesitated and then explained what had happened. He paused before asking, *Have any of you ever jumped off anything? Like a huge, moving ship?*

The stingrays stared at him questioningly.

I mean, if you had to, do you think you would survive jumping from this ship to go get help?

Are you nuts, bobo? one of the stingrays asked him.

Sorry, Tristan said quickly. He turned to the two spotted eagle rays in the tank. *What about you?*

We jump—pretty high, too, said an eagle ray. *But not from so high up. Sorry; even though we don't have any bones to break, we'd be done for, hagfish food, crab bait . . .*

I get it, Tristan thought before the ray could go on. He then thanked them anyway and joined Sam. Hugh had just climbed out of another tank.

"Nope, the rays are out," Tristan told them.

"What about the fish?" Sam asked Hugh.

"No way," Hugh responded. "They said that squashed and chopped-up, very dead fish wouldn't be much help to anyone."

"Now what?" Sam muttered.

"Hold on," Hugh said. "The fish may not want to jump, but there are some big sea stars in the tank, and one said it would go. They think it'll make it. Sea stars have tough skin, are full of water, and have no bones to break. And if this one loses an arm or two in the fall, they'll just grow back."

"Not if—as you say—it gets chopped up by the propellers," Tristan noted.

"We need to find a way to help it fall away from the ship," Sam suggested. "But there's another problem. It could take days for a sea star to crawl to Ozdale's yacht. No offense to the sea stars."

"Oh, it doesn't want to be the messenger," Hugh told them. "The sea star suggested we get a fish to go

with it. To sit on the sea star's sticky feet and the sea
star will break the fall."

"Did any of the fish in the tank agree to that?"
Tristan asked.

"No," Hugh answered. "Most say they're too big.
But I know one that would fit perfectly."

20

THE JUMP

THE CAYMAN COAST GUARD DROPPED COACH
Fred and Ms. Sanchez off at Ozdale's yacht. The com-
mander apologized that they couldn't do more. The
Dawn Oasis was free to leave Grand Cayman.

After the Coast Guard left, Coach gathered the
others. "Looks like a fully armed search or confisca-
tion of the ship are out. The authorities here simply
have no backbone."

"Or they have actual laws that need to be followed,"
Ms. Sanchez noted.

Rosina raised her hand.

"Yes, Gonzales?" Coach asked.

"Coach, while you were on the ship, we found
some birds."

"And?"

"They offered to help."

"And?"

"It's a group of royal terns. At least, that's what they said they are. They flew over to the ship and organized a landing party. And one found Hugh hiding in a small boat on deck."

"That's good news, right?" Ozdale asked hopefully.

"Well, it confirms that they're onboard and alive," Coach said.

"Should we call the Coast Guard back?" Ozdale asked.

Coach shook his head. "No use there. I don't think they'll take it very seriously if we say a little birdie told us the campers are on the ship."

"It was a stretch just to get them to stop the cargo ship by showing them the tracking signals, which appear to be coming from somewhere aboard," Ms. Sanchez added.

"Looks like it is up to us to stop that vessel," Coach noted.

"How are we going to do that?" Ryder asked dubiously.

No one spoke for a few very quiet minutes. Then Coach raised his eyebrows and turned to Ozdale. "About those inventions of yours. Do you have insurance?"

In the cargo ship's hidden hold, the teens prepared for launch. They found a big cooler to transport the volunteers from the holding tanks up to the ship's open deck.

"So, any ideas on how to avoid a sea-star splatter against the ship's hull?" Tristan asked Sam and Hugh quietly. He knew the sea star couldn't understand him, but still, he didn't want to say it too loudly.

"If only Ozdale were here," Hugh replied. "He could probably invent something to help."

"Ozdale," Sam said, her eyes widening. "I know. We need a parachute."

"A parachute?" Tristan said. "Great idea, but where are we going to get a sea-star parachute?"

"Not get one," Hugh noted, nodding his head. "Make one. We can use line from the nets, and then we just need some sort of light material."

Tristan looked around for something they could use. Sam was staring at Hugh, smirking mischievously.

"What? What are you looking at?" Hugh asked.

"Your shorts," Sam answered.

"What about my shorts?"

"Yeah, they're perfect," Tristan said. "The material is light, and we can tie up the legs so they'll hold air."

"My swimsuit? You want to use it as a parachute?" Hugh asked dubiously. "Why my shorts? What about yours? Besides, I am not running around here naked."

Sam laughed and ran over to where Hugh's wetsuit from earlier lay. She picked it up and tossed it to him. "Take off your shorts and put this back on."

Hugh turned to Tristan. "How about using your shorts?"

"I still have my wetsuit on, and we need to get

moving. Besides, yours will be wider, if you know what
I mean, and hold more air. No offense or anything."

Hugh shook his head, shrugging. "Okay, okay. You
guys cut some line from the nets while I change." He
tossed Tristan the stingray barb to use as a knife and
turned to Sam. "And *no* looking."

Tristan and Sam scampered across the catwalks to
a pile of netting. After they had cut what looked like
enough line from the nets, they ran back to Hugh. He
had the wetsuit back on and was holding his swimsuit.
They quickly tied a piece of line tightly around each
pant leg and then poked holes just below the short's
waistband. Then they tied a couple of longer lengths
to the waistband. They held up their creation—a very
strange-looking parachute.

"Think it'll work?" Sam asked.

"Maybe," Tristan answered skeptically.

The teens put water from a tank into the cooler.
Hugh collected the sea star volunteer. It was pumpkin
orange, had five wide arms, and was about eight inches
across. He placed the sea star gently in the water in the
cooler. "It says to tie the shorts—I mean parachute—to
it upside down, wants to land on its top."

Tristan and Sam tied the parachute's lines to the sea
star's arms using slipknots so the creature could dump
the thing once it landed. Meanwhile, Hugh went cautiously into the shark tank to collect their other fishy
recruit. He came back carrying the soon-to-be remora
paratrooper.

"Says this must be its destiny," Hugh told them.

"After all, remoras are the ultimate team players, always relying on others. Hanging on. Going headfirst . . . stuck onboard."

Tristan and Sam rolled their eyes at Hugh's terrible jokes.

"Hey, I'm just telling you what it said."

Hugh carefully put the remora in the transport cooler. He placed it on the upside-down sea star, whose hundreds of suction-cupped tube feet created a sticky cushion for the small fish. The remora squirmed and Hugh chuckled.

"What's so funny?" Sam asked.

"Says it tickles," Hugh told them.

"Okay, let's do this," Tristan urged them, trying to sound confident. Tristan wasn't happy about possibly sending two sea creatures to their doom. But they had to try something. And this was the only plan, crazy as it was, that they had come up with.

Sam ran ahead to open the sliding steel wall. Tristan and Hugh followed, carrying the cooler. They tried not to slosh the contents around too much to prevent beating up their potential sea-creature superheroes, or making them queasy before they even got to the side of the ship. Sam took the lead and acted as lookout. They moved as quietly and as quickly as possible to the metal staircases that led up to the cargo ship's open deck. It was awkward carrying the cooler up the stairs and slowgoing as they tried not to turn it into a marine-life washing machine.

At the top of the final set of stairs, Sam crept out

and looked around. "Coast's clear. Let's do this fast and then get back out of sight."

Hugh and Tristan nodded. Carrying the cooler, the two boys followed Sam, staying low. The three of them stopped at a spot between the ship's rail and a stack of giant cargo containers sitting on deck. Tristan squinted in the bright morning sun. No one seemed to be around. He stood up, and wind from the ship's motion blasted his face. Tristan turned aft, gazing behind the ship. George Town was barely visible now. The ship was cruising steadily away from the only land around. Tristan leaned over the rail. Far below, the water churned and rushed past the hull. He cringed at the thought of anyone or anything jumping.

Hugh opened the cooler and gingerly picked up the remora-carrying sea star. Tristan and Sam untangled the lines of the upside-down shorts parachute and held it up.

"Okay, on three," Tristan said quietly, praying their absurd plan would work, or at least not painfully murder their volunteers.

"Good luck," Hugh said.

"You can do it," Sam added, even though the creatures wouldn't understand her.

"One, two, and *three!*"

Tristan and Sam opened the waistband of the shorts as wide as possible. Then, just as Hugh gently tossed the sea creatures off the ship, they released the shorts. Immediately, the sea star began to plummet downward toward the ship's hull.

"Oh, crap," Tristan groaned.

It looked like it was going to be the rapid dive of death, a quick and fatal splatter against the ship's hull. The three teens watched in dismay. Tristan felt a heavy knot in the pit of his stomach. Then, a gust of wind hit the shorts. The funky parachute filled with air and rose up. Soon their sea-creature paratroopers were floating gently away from the ship and down toward the sea.

"Yahoo! It's working," Tristan shouted. Then, remembering where he was, Tristan slapped a hand over his mouth and crouched down on the deck.

"C'mon, let's find a way to slow this thing down," Sam urged, running back to the stairwell.

Leaving the cooler behind, Tristan and Hugh followed.

On the bridge, three stories above the open deck, the helmsman stared out the windows toward the bow. He saw a flicker of movement and something fly off the ship from behind a stack of crates. It looked like a bird or a random piece of trash whipped up in the wind. But something unusual about the motion caught his eye. He reached for a pair of high-powered binoculars. "What the heck?"

He turned to the first officer. "Uh, sir, I know this sounds crazy, but I swear I just saw some shorts fly off the ship."

The officer responded with a look questioning the man's sanity. "What?" he then laughed. "Is Iggy running around in his birthday suit down there? Now *that* is not a sight I want to see."

"I'm serious, sir. Come look for yourself," the helmsman said.

The first officer walked over, shaking his head. He grabbed the binoculars. As he tried to focus on the small dot floating down and away from the ship, a puzzled look spread across his face. "What in the world?"

The man walked calmly to the wide flat-screen that showed the feeds from the ship's security cameras. He punched up the image for the camera in the hidden hold. It was still off from the inspection. They hadn't wanted someone mistakenly bringing the image up while the authorities were aboard. He cursed and switched the camera on. An image popped up, but it was not what he expected. It was all fuzzy and gray, as if the camera was engulfed in a blizzard of dirty snow. "We'd better send someone down there to check it out. Also, we're not too far away yet—call our partner onshore and have him investigate whatever just went over the side."

21

COLLISION COURSE

Tristan, Hugh, and Sam ran down several flights of stairs to a lower deck. They crouched against the wall in another of the wide metal passageways that ran the length of the ship.

"Now what?" Hugh whispered. "Any ideas?"

"Maybe we can do something to the engines," Tristan suggested.

"We don't know where the engine room is," Sam said. "And besides, I bet there'll be more of the stink crew there."

Hugh nodded. "We could find a place to hide and hope the remora gets our message to the others. Assuming it survived, of course."

The more he thought about it, the more Tristan doubted their message-by-remora plan would work.

They needed another plan—with any luck, a better one, and one that didn't include the strong probability of killing those involved. *C'mon,* Tristan said to himself. *Think of something.* Here was his chance to make up for getting them into this situation in the first place. He thought back to everything they'd done and seen on the ship—starting at when they first got dragged into the bow. "The bow!"

"What about it?" Hugh asked.

"Remember those big doors that opened up and sucked us in?" Tristan said.

"Yeah," Hugh responded. "Pretty hard to forget."

"Wonder what would happen if they started to open while the ship is moving?"

"Why didn't I think of that?" Sam said. "They'd have to stop the ship. Then we could swim out." She hugged Tristan. "That's brilliant!"

Tristan grinned, suddenly feeling much better about everything. "Do you guys remember how to get there?"

Hugh shook his head and then paused. "Hey, wait. The way into the bow was on the same deck as the opening into the secret hold with all the tanks."

"Yeah, you're right," Tristan said. "And it's probably hidden or something."

"C'mon," Sam whispered, as she left the shadows and headed for the stairs going down. Tristan and Hugh followed. Suddenly, a red light on a nearby wall began flashing and a high-pitched alarm sounded.

"Uh-oh," Sam said. "I think they've discovered that we're no longer resting uncomfortably in that tank."

"Hurry!" Tristan urged, running down another flight of stairs.

On the bridge, Captain Johnson was like a lioness deprived of a fresh kill. She paced back and forth, glaring at the officers and crew. "Can't you idiots do anything right? What kind of a lamebrain crew is this? A couple of kids, and you can't even hold on to 'em."

"Uh, Captain, sir?" said the first officer.

"Now what?" she answered, with a look that would make Superman run for the hills.

"I've got several vessels approaching on radar. One is our Cayman guy investigating what went over the side. But the other two are unknowns. And one of them is all over the map, zig-zagging, doing circles— totally off the wall."

"'Totally off the wall'? Is that your detailed nautical analysis? Where did you get your training, the Maritime Academy for Morons?"

"No, sir. Of course not, sir. It's just that it looks funny to me."

"It looks *funny* to you?" the captain growled as she walked angrily to the radar screen. A small blip indicated a boat was trailing the ship on the starboard side. On the port side, the screen showed another two blips. One appeared to be a small boat heading steadily for them, but the other target was moving in fits and starts, weaving crazily. At one point it even did a donut, going round and round in a nearly stationary circle.

The captain grabbed the binoculars and searched for the vessels to their port. "Officer, get on the horn and warn those boats off. They're headed into our cruising path."

"Yes, sir."

"Any word on the search for the kids?"

"No, sir."

"Why am I not surprised?" She added, "If we're lucky, they jumped off the ship to a quick and particularly agonizing death. Call our friend in the small boat to see if he's found any blood or remains in the water."

At the helm of the skiff *Little Green*, Coach Fred stayed well behind Ozdale. "I know he insisted on driving, but that man has to be the worst driver I've ever seen."

"He'll be fine," Ms. Sanchez said uncertainly. "Besides, it's his hovercraft, and this will undoubtedly be his last ride in it. Given what you've asked him to do."

"Well, let's just hope he sticks to the plan." Coach picked up the radio. "*Hover One*, come in."

"Go ahead, Coach," Ryder responded on the radio.

"Jones, see if you can get Ozdale to drive anywhere near straight. About another quarter mile to go, and then you know what to do."

"Roger that, Coach."

"You and Gonzales ready?"

"Yes, Coach."

"Okay. We'll be off your stern and standing by."

The sharp-pitched buzzing of the alarm made even thinking hard. The flashing lights didn't help, especially in a place surrounded by bright red steel. Tristan felt like he was in a no-fun fun house. He, Hugh, and Sam sprinted down the stairs to the deck with the hidden cargo hold. Tristan was about to bust out into the passageway and head to the bow when Sam grabbed his arm, pulled him back, and put a finger to her lips.

A voice echoed down the passageway. "We'll work our way back. Them brats are here somewhere, and we'll find 'em—or heads will roll."

Tristan recognized the voice—Tiny.

"I like my head where it is," whined Iggy.

The teens tiptoed up a few stairs and flattened themselves against the wall.

"Stop your moaning and get moving," Tiny said, jogging aft.

They stopped just outside the stairwell.

"Which way?" Iggy asked.

"Junior is up a deck with Toolman. We're going aft. Didn't I just say that?"

"Did you?" Iggy muttered.

Tristan's heart was pounding so hard he thought for sure the two men would hear it. He tried to stay absolutely still and breathe as little as possible.

"C'mon, dog breath," Tiny growled. "Get a move on."

The men's footsteps faded as they headed toward the ship's stern. The three teens crept down the stairs. They peered cautiously into the passageway to be sure the men were gone. After exiting the stairwell, the campers made their way forward to the steel wall at the end of the passageway. It was a dead end—or what looked like a dead end. While they were searching for a hidden latch or button, the ship's alarm abruptly went silent and the flashing lights stopped.

A voice boomed over the ship's intercom. "Tiny to the bridge, on the double. Crew, prepare for collision."

Tristan turned to Hugh and Sam, thinking, *That can't be good.* "Uh, guys, maybe going into the bow isn't such a great idea if the ship is about to crash into something?"

Sam and Hugh nodded. The three teens stood unmoving, unsure of where to go or what to do next. Their new plan had gone from sounding pretty good to probably deadly.

Tiny entered the bridge with Iggy trailing behind. The two men were huffing as if they'd just run a marathon.

"You called, Captain?" Tiny gasped.

"What's going on?" Iggy added, bent over and breathing hard.

Captain Johnson glared at Iggy like she wanted to

pitch him overboard. She turned to the man at the helm. "Slow her down so those lunatics can cross our path. Last thing we need now is an accident to bring out the authorities again. And give another blast of the horn."

"Yes, sir. Slowing," the helmsman said, right before letting off another blast of the ship's horn.

"Tiny, call and see what our local friend has found. I want to know what went overboard back there. First officer, what are those other boats doing?"

While the first officer stared through the binoculars, Tiny pulled a cell phone from his pocket and punched in a number.

"Captain," the first officer replied, "The boat in front, if you could call it that, is still heading straight—no, make that sort of winding—into our cruise path. The other boat appears to be hanging back, coming on more slowly."

"Give me those," the Captain ordered, grabbing the binoculars from the officer. "What the crap is that thing? Don't they know we'll turn 'em into scrap metal?"

"Captain, ma'am," Iggy said. "I mean, sir. Let me look."

The captain returned Iggy's request with a steely stare.

"Or not," he said. "Just thought I might be able to identify the vessel."

"Oh, why not," the captain moaned, handing the binoculars to Iggy.

"It's a hovercraft," Iggy shouted. "Very cool!"

The captain smacked Iggy across the side of the head.

Iggy rubbed his head. "Hey, what was that for? It's not like you see a hovercraft every day."

Tiny had walked over to the captain. "Sir, the only thing he found was some swim trunks floating on the surface."

The first officer and helmsman exchanged a knowing glance.

"Ah, Captain," Iggy then said. "He's not slowing down or changing course."

The captain turned to the helmsman. "Okay. If this moron wants to play chicken, bring it on. Steady on your course."

"But, Captain," said the helmsman. "What about..."

"Are you questioning my orders?" the captain asked menacingly. "Do we have a problem here?" She stroked the whip at her hip almost lovingly.

"Uh, no, sir."

Captain Johnson turned to Tiny. "You and Iggy go to the bow. If we hit 'em, we'll stop to remove the evidence. And when I say 'remove,' I mean make sure that vessel and anyone inside it takes a quick, deep dive to the bottom."

22

BIRD SERVICE

Tristan, Sam, and Hugh decided to go back up to the open deck to see what the ship was about to crash into. They crept cautiously up stairways and along passageways. Wanting to avoid the crew, the teens sniffed the air as they went. They figured the crew's horrid stench would give them away, even at a distance. At one point, they heard pounding footsteps headed their way. The teens hunkered down in a dark stairwell until the men had passed.

When they reached the open deck, Sam was the first to peek out. "Clear."

The three of them moved stealthily out to the rail, keeping as low as possible. They rose up just enough to look over the side of the ship.

"I don't see anything," Tristan said.

"Me either," Hugh added.

Another deafening blast of the ship's horn made them jump.

"C'mon, let's go closer to the bow and look from there," Tristan suggested.

Hugh and Sam nervously agreed. They all crept forward, trying to stay low and hidden among the stacks of cargo containers on deck. Sam suddenly stopped, plugged her nose, and made a face. Tristan smelled it too. One of the crew was nearby, his stench tainting the air like cologne-de-ogre. They stopped and smelled in different directions. Sam pointed ahead and to the right of one of the cargo crates. The three teens snuck around to the left, keeping the crate between themselves and the thuggish crew member. Once the stink dissipated and they were sure he had gone the other way, Sam, Tristan, and Hugh continued moving toward the bow.

They came to a large white cylindrical container sitting in a cradle next to the rail. It was a life raft. The teens crouched down behind it. Tristan looked aft and up to the row of windows across the bridge. If they stood up now, they'd easily be seen by anyone looking down from the bridge.

A piercing, spine-shivering screech then ripped through the air. It sounded like a thousand fingernails scraping down a blackboard and was followed by the sound of crunching metal. The ship's engines immediately went silent.

Tristan couldn't resist. As inconspicuously as possible, he rose to a scrunched-over position and scrambled to the raised lip of the bow. He stood up and peered over the side. "Oh, no." He quickly dropped down and crawled to where Sam and Hugh were still hiding. "It's Ozdale's hovercraft. The ship just smashed into it. It's all crumpled up and looks like it's jammed onto the bow."

"Was anyone inside it?" Sam asked worriedly.

"Couldn't see anyone. But if they were, it's not good."

Inside the ship's hidden bow compartment, Tiny and two other crew members were readying three sets of scuba gear.

"As soon as the ship stops, open the doors," Tiny yelled to Iggy, who was at the top of the stairs that led down into the hidden compartment. Tiny turned to the other divers and handed each a speargun, along with an underwater blowtorch for cutting through metal. "Let's make this quick, boys, before anyone comes to investigate."

"What if there are survivors?" one man asked.

Tiny held up a speargun. The other two grinned and nodded, as if they couldn't wait for a little under-sea target practice. The men slung their scuba tanks over their backs.

When the ship had nearly stopped, Tiny shouted, "Now!"

Iggy hit a button, and the cargo ship's huge bow doors began to slowly swing open. He then flicked a switch to the up position to turn the intake pumps on. Water poured into the bow. The three divers jumped and swam out beneath the surface.

Meanwhile, several decks up, the three teens heard the mechanical hum of the doors opening. Tristan dared another peek over the side. He ducked back down. "The bow is opening and the hovercraft is stuck on one of the doors."

"What should we do?" Hugh asked in a whisper.

No one said anything. Tristan wondered if they should try to make a run for the bow and swim out while the doors were open. Did they have enough time? Would there be more crew down there? It didn't seem like a very good option.

"Did you see anyone in the water, or other boats out there?" Sam asked.

Tristan shook his head.

"Maybe we should jump," Hugh suggested.

Tristan stared at his friend openmouthed.

"Jump?" Sam whispered. "Aren't you the one who said it'd be the leap of death? Splattered and then chopped up?"

Hugh nodded. "Yeah, but the ship has stopped, and, well, I've reconsidered my previous analysis. We might survive. And with the hovercraft down there, the others must be out there waiting or looking for us. Or they will be soon. Besides, I've had enough of this ship. I want off—now."

"*Might survive?*" Sam questioned.

Hugh shrugged. "Hey, that's better than 'I'm 100 percent sure we'll die.' Besides, I've seen people jump out of helicopters into the ocean."

"Yeah," Tristan replied. "On TV."

"And those were trained rescue divers or Navy SEALs," Sam added.

"Have a better idea?" Hugh asked.

Both Tristan and Sam shook their heads.

"Let's go back a bit. It looks lower there," Hugh told them.

Staying low, they crept slowly back to about midship, in preparation for a jump that could very well be their last.

The divers exited the bow and turned left toward the smashed hovercraft. They looked inside the crumpled hunk of acrylic, fiberglass, and metal for bodies. Not that it would make a difference. One diver then stood on lookout. Tiny and the other man began using their underwater blowtorches to cut through the remains of the hovercraft to ensure a speedy trip to the seafloor.

Within seconds, the diver on lookout grabbed Tiny's arm. He pointed into the blue water surrounding them. Tiny squinted, obviously trying to figure out what the man was pointing at. Something was coming toward them. It took a moment for Tiny to realize what it was. Then it was all too clear. A giant mouth full of dagger-sharp serrated teeth was headed directly toward him. Tiny brought up his speargun. Another extremely large shark came into view. It was surrounded by a pack of smaller sharks. As the sharks swam toward them, the divers quit what they were doing and huddled back to back. Tiny pointed to the ship. Without looking back, all three divers swam for it as fast as they could. Tiny tried to aim and fire his speargun. But one of the sharks gave a sharp yank on Tiny's fins, sending the spear sailing harmlessly off into open water. The men entered the bow and swam hard for the ladder. The sharks remained just outside, circling and gnashing their teeth threateningly. Tiny scrambled up to the platform in the compartment. He spit out his regulator. "What the heck?"

"Did you sink it?" Iggy asked.

"Didn't have a chance," Tiny growled. "Shark attack."

A voice rang out over an intercom in the bow compartment. "Has our little problem been taken care of, boys?" It was the captain.

Iggy picked up the ship's phone from the wall. "No, ma'am. I mean, sir . . . a problem with sharks."

"Sharks?"

"Yes, sir."

"Well, kill 'em and get that thing off my bow."

Iggy passed the message on to Tiny and the two divers. The divers refused to get back in the water. Tiny stared at the sharks circling in front of the open bow. It was a toss-up: queen of mean or giant tiger sharks. He stayed where he was.

Tristan was sitting on deck about midship, taking deep breaths and trying to build up his courage. His hands were trembling. Sweat trickled down his neck. Fear seemed to have crept into every pore of his body. No way to channel or suppress it this time. He was scared stiff. They were going to do it. They were going to jump off the cargo ship. It had to be at least four stories high. Sam sat nearby, nervously twirling her hair. Hugh had turned whiter than an albino dolphin.

"You really think we'll survive it?" Sam asked Hugh.

"Maybe," Hugh answered. "Definitely some broken bones, maybe a collapsed lung, and possibly paralysis due to a spinal injury."

Tristan stared at Hugh. "That's *not* very encouraging."

"Do you want me to lie?"

"Yes!" said Sam and Tristan simultaneously.

"In case we don't make it," Tristan said. "I just want you guys to know I'm really sorry. Hugh, you were right, we should have found a way off the ship first thing. I should have listened to you. You guys are the best friends I've ever had. And Sam, I—"

Just then, a large shadow fell over the teens. Tristan looked up, thinking it was Tiny or another member of the stink crew. It wasn't. But it took a moment for him to make sense of what he was seeing. Two big black birds were flying overhead. Each bird had a white chest, wide wingspan, and forked tail. Tristan recognized them: frigatebirds. And they were carrying something. From where Tristan sat, it looked dark and rectangular. He couldn't tell exactly what it was. The birds then released their payload, and a dark-green duffle bag landed with a thud nearly on top of Hugh. Tristan hurriedly grabbed it and slid it toward them, thinking someone on the bridge probably saw the big-bird delivery service. Written across the duffle in large white letters was *Ozdale Industries.*

Tristan grinned and unzipped the duffle. On top was an instruction card, which he read out loud: "Emergency Kevlar Rescue Chute. Place hooks securely on window edge or rail, roll chute out, and pull CO_2 cartridge cord to inflate. While sliding down, keep hands and feet in and crossed. Use at your own risk. Severe injuries or death are possible, along with broken legs, arms, ribs, and nose. Cuts, bruises, and skin rashes are likely."

From further aft came the thud of footsteps and men shouting. The teens hurriedly placed the hooks over the ship's rail. Then they pushed the rolled-up chute off the ship.

"Hope this one's been fully tested," Hugh said as he pulled the inflate cord.

A loud hissing sound emanated from a canister attached to the underside of the rescue chute as it inflated. The teens glanced over the side of the ship. It looked like a long amusement-park slide ending a couple feet above the water.

"Ladies first," Tristan said.

Without hesitation, Sam climbed onto a box on the deck, then to the rail, and leapt feetfirst into the inflated rescue chute. She crossed her legs and arms as if she was going down a long, steep waterslide. Sam zoomed down the chute and then shot out over the water, away from the ship. She bounced several times and did a somersault. It wasn't the most graceful of landings.

Looking aft, Tristan saw three men running their way. He urged Hugh to slide down next and prayed he'd have enough time to follow. Hugh climbed up onto the box. Tristan was right behind him. Hugh hesitated. He and Tristan glanced back. The big, stinky crewmen were closing in.

"Go!" shouted Tristan, giving Hugh an encouraging shove.

Hugh jumped/fell into the chute. Tristan wanted to jump in too, but if he went too soon, he'd land on top of Hugh. Time slowed as he waited for Hugh to slide down the chute. Seconds seemed like hours. Tristan's heart was pounding. He could smell the men approaching. It was going to be close. Getting ready to jump, Tristan glanced back. One of the stink men was right there, reaching for him. Suddenly, all Tristan saw was flapping black feathers. A frigatebird was pecking at the man's nose. The malodorous lug stopped, cursed, and swatted at the bird. The rest of the crew dove for cover behind a stack of containers.

Tristan jumped into the rescue chute and bounced. He thought for sure he was going to career right over the side. But thankfully, he landed back on it and flew straight down. Air rushed up at him, and his wetsuit began to ride up, super-wedgie style. Tristan then remembered the instructions. He crossed his arms and legs. He felt like he was free-falling. He shot off the end of the chute, hit the water, and bounced again, landing hard on his butt. It felt like he'd hit concrete. *That's going to leave a mark*, Tristan thought. He looked back and saw a bunch of smaller, white-and-gray birds with funky hairdos pecking holes in the chute. It deflated with a loud blubbering sound and lay limp against the cargo ship's hull. Now none of the crew could follow them into the water. Tristan silently thanked the birds.

The three teens swam fast. Once a sufficient distance away from the cargo ship, they gathered on the surface, treading water. Tristan heard a familiar sound and spun around. A small boat was speeding toward them. Ryder and Rosina were at the bow, waving. Coach Fred was driving, with Ms. Sanchez and Ozdale at his side. Minutes later, Tristan, Sam, and Hugh were gratefully being helped into the skiff.

23

JAMMED OPEN

As soon as the teens were safely in the small boat, Ozdale turned to them excitedly. "How was the ride down?"

"Awesome!" Tristan answered. "Thanks, Mr. Ozdale; you really saved our butts."

"Like you all did for me in Monterey—and please, call me Leo. Nothing better than seeing one of my inventions work *and* save lives. I couldn't be happier."

"But what about your hovercraft?" Hugh asked.

"Oh, a minor casualty. I can always build another one."

"How'd you get out without being crushed?" Sam questioned.

Ozdale turned to Rosina and Ryder. "Had a little help there. We ditched into the ocean right before the collision, and these two helped me swim back here underwater."

Ryder nodded proudly. "And while we were swimming back, those tiger sharks showed up. Not like we knew what they were saying or anything, but there was this weird little fish attached to one of them."

Ms. Sanchez interjected, "The remora you sent. It actually tried to leap right into the boat, so I got in the water and that crazy little fish stuck right onto my forehead. It said you were unhurt but still trapped onboard. When the bow doors started opening, we thought maybe you three would be there getting ready to swim out. The sharks left, and we figured they went to watch for you."

"That's when the birds reported seeing you on deck again," Rosina said. "One saw you earlier, Hugh."

Hugh rubbed his head. "Yeah, I know."

"After that, they took shifts circling above the ship, watching for you guys."

"The special delivery was Miss Rosina's idea," Ozdale said. "She remembered seeing the rescue chute bag on the yacht."

That's when Tristan did something that surprised everybody, even himself. He ran to Rosina and hugged her. "Thank you. Thank you." He was just so relieved to be off the ship, alive, and not responsible for the horrible deaths of his two best friends.

Rosina looked shocked after Tristan released her. "Uh, yeah, sure."

"Yeah, thanks," Sam added. "And to the birds, too. We were about to jump for it."

"Enough chitchat," Coach announced. "I've radi-
oed the Cayman Coast Guard about the hovercraft
'accident.' They say if the ship gets into international
waters before they can get there, there's not much they
can do other than report it to the International Maritime Authorities."

As they were talking, a small boat cruised into view.
It came around the cargo ship's stern. The ship's bow
doors then began to slowly close.

"We've got to stop them," Tristan said. "They've got
this big, secret hold with huge tanks. They're full of sea
creatures. The missing stingrays are there, along with
some sharks and a bunch of other animals."

"And the tanks are way too small," said Sam. "It's
terrible. And who knows where they're taking them."

"Collectors, I bet. *Illegal* collectors," Ms. Sanchez
said. "I hate these guys." She pulled a cell phone off the
steering console and looked to Coach Fred. "May I?"

"Be my guest. Let's tell the Coast Guard exactly
what is on that ship. Where is that hidden hold, Hunt?"

Tristan, Sam, and Hugh described the location of
the secret cargo hold. As they talked, the rumble of the
cargo ship's engines echoed across the water. They all
turned to watch as the bow doors continued to close.
The ship was preparing to get back underway. The
other small boat stayed away but seemed to be shadowing them. It looked like the driver was talking on a
phone or radio.

Staying a safe distance away, Coach steered their
boat toward the cargo ship's bow. Tristan stared at the
remains of the hovercraft. It was still stuck on one of

the bow doors. That gave him an idea. "Coach, what if we can keep the bow doors from closing all the way?"

Coach Fred thought for a moment. "I see where you're going, Hunt. If the bow doors are open and they get underway, water will flood in. Probably won't sink them, but might be enough to either stop or slow the ship down."

Staring at the hovercraft wreckage, Hugh said, "Yeah, but all they have to do is push that thing off from the inside."

"Not if we jam it in real tight," Coach offered. "But we need to move quickly, before the doors close all the way. Are you up for it, campers?"

"Yes!"

"Okay, hop in. And Hunt, keep your eyes open for those sharks. I thought I saw some fins still circling near the ship. They might be able to help."

Ms. Sanchez handed Tristan, Sam, and Hugh each an algae-water pill and some water. They downed the pills gladly. Moments later, the teens slid into the water. Just before they swam off, Ozdale waved Tristan over. He handed him his shiny silver cane. "It's made of a special titanium alloy I developed for my deep-diving sub. If you can jam this in there too, it can withstand huge amounts of pressure."

Tristan looked at the man questioningly, not sure if he should take his cane.

"Go ahead, take it," Ozdale urged.

Carrying Ozdale's cane, Tristan swam to catch up to the other teens swimming toward the cargo ship's bow. A shadow to his right drew his attention. Soon, a large tiger shark was swimming beside him. Another tiger shark and a pack of blacktips followed.

Relief washed over Tristan and he smiled at the lead tiger shark. *Glad to see you're okay. I thought you'd, you know, bit the big one back there.*

Nice to see you too, the shark told him. *I was a little out of it for a while after getting knocked unconscious. But I'm good now. Sharks have excellent healing abilities.*

Hey, me too, Tristan thought. *And we found your missing cousins, along with the stingrays. They're all trapped inside some tanks hidden in the ship.*

The shark nodded its head. *Yeah, we figured it out based on what we could understand from that remora you sent.* The shark opened and closed its mouth angrily. *Now there are some humans I'd like to take a bite out of!*

Tristan then explained what they were planning to do. The sharks wanted to help.

The five teens, along with two large tiger sharks, a pack of blacktips, and one very small remora on a ride-along, arrived at the smashed-up hovercraft, still stuck on the door. The bow doors had about thirty feet to go before they would be fully closed. One of the tiger sharks swam up to the mashed hovercraft. It opened its mouth like it was about to start chewing on the wreckage.

Tristan swam over to the shark and gently tapped it on the head, staying well away from its teeth. *Hey, we're supposed to push it in further, not try to eat the thing.*

Sorry, said the shark. *Bad habit.*

Tristan shrugged good-naturedly at the shark and then demonstrated pushing on the wreckage. The group encircled the vehicle's remains. They had to time it perfectly. If they pushed too soon and the hovercraft came off the bow door, it would sink to the bottom. The doors were now about twenty feet apart and still closing. Tristan paused, signaling the others to wait to start pushing. When the bow doors were about fifteen feet apart, he nodded and motioned to push.

The entire team, humans and sharks together, shoved hard on the wreckage. It didn't budge. They pushed harder. Tristan felt a little movement. He kicked his feet, pushing with all his might. The sharks whipped their powerful tails back and forth. Tristan heard the screech of metal on metal. The wreckage twisted and began to slide. The doors were still closing. They were only ten feet apart. Tristan thought of all the animals trapped inside the ship and pushed harder.

Then, just as the doors were about to close all the way, a section of the wrecked hovercraft slid forward. A loud crash resounded as the bow doors smashed into it. The team let go and jumped back. A portion of the wreckage was now jammed in, and the bow doors were stuck open. Tristan swam carefully under the once spaceship-like hovercraft. He found a perfectly sized space and crammed Ozdale's titanium-alloy cane between the doors. He wedged it in tight. While he was working, Tristan could feel the doors still trying to close.

The teens and sharks gave the wreckage one last shove to be sure it was firmly wedged in and then swam back to the skiff. Before he got out of the water,

Tristan made a suggestion to the sharks. He watched as two huge fins rose out of the water and headed for the other small boat still shadowing their skiff. The man at the boat's helm saw the fins and began to veer away. The fins followed. Soon the small boat was speeding toward shore.

On the bridge, the captain's face had turned scarily scarlet as she barked into the ship's phone. "Iggy, you imbecile. What is going on down there? We're ready to depart. Are the bow doors closed?"

"Ma'am, sir, uh, we've run into another little problem."

"Captain, Iggy. Just Captain. One more, 'ma'am,' and it'll be your last. What is going on down there?"

"Uh, well. The wrecked hovercraft is sort of, well, now jammed between the doors."

"What? You tell Tiny that if he values his life, he'll get that hunk of junk off my ship now!"

"Captain. He's trying, but it seems to be stuck."

"Iggy. It'll be both of your heads if we are not moving in two minutes."

"Yes . . . Captain," Iggy muttered. "I . . . I think they're making progress. I'm sure the doors will be closed any second now."

After he hung up the phone, Iggy stared at where the divers were still trying unsuccessfully to free the

doors and shut the bow. In truth, it didn't look any
better than before, but he wasn't about to tell the captain that. He really did like his head where it was.

Captain Johnson turned to the crew in the bridge.
"I want everything ready to go. Two minutes from
now, we're going full speed ahead and leaving this
sorry place."

The crew looked nervously at one another and then
prepared the ship for departure.

Coach Fred steered the boat away from the cargo ship
as they waited to see what would happen. The ship
then began to move slowly forward.

"Looks like someone is getting impatient," Coach
Fred said.

"Can they move with the bow partly open like
that?" Sam asked.

The cargo ship began to pick up speed. Maybe
they'd been wrong, Tristan thought. Maybe the ship
could cruise, even with the bow doors jammed open.

"How far till international waters?" Ms. Sanchez
asked.

The men inside the bow compartment were scrambling. The wrecked hovercraft remained wedged

tightly between the bow doors. The crew tried to open the doors in hopes that the trashed vehicle would slide off and sink. But now the doors wouldn't close fully or open further. The wreckage was solidly stuck in place and the doors were jammed open. With the ship now moving, water was flooding into the bow fast. Having just escaped being smashed up against the platform by surging seawater, Tiny scrambled up the ladder, taking the rungs two at a time. He shoved Iggy out of the way and grabbed the phone from a cradle on the wall. "Captain, stop the ship. Stop the ship! The bow's flooding fast."

"What?" screamed the voice over the phone. "I thought you just about had the bow doors closed."

"Who told you that?" the huge man snarled. He turned to where Iggy cowered in the shadows and then spoke again into the phone, "Yes, sir, we'll try the pumps, but I don't think they can keep up with the inflow."

Tiny switched on the pumps, and Iggy headed for the exit from the bow.

"Where do you think you're going?" Tiny growled menacingly.

The cargo ship continued to head offshore, but it had slowed to a near creep and the bow plowed down as if pulled by a giant weight. Tristan and the others watched from the skiff. The ship wasn't sinking, but it also wasn't going anywhere anytime soon. Then they heard sirens and saw the flashing lights of three Cayman Coast Guard vessels approaching.

"Looks like the cavalry has arrived," Ms. Sanchez noted with a grin.

"Perfect timing," Hugh added.

As they watched, two men jumped from the cargo ship. One was noticeably huge and the other scrawny and particularly disheveled.

"Looks like our friend Tiny decided to go for a swim," Tristan said, laughing. He couldn't help but enjoy thinking about how much the landing must have hurt. He rubbed his sore butt. The smaller of the two men was dragged out of the water unconscious. The other seemed to have withstood the fall. But once he started swimming for shore, several very large fins began circling the man. Compared to the sharks, even Tiny looked small and pathetic. The man stopped and waved frantically to the Coast Guard vessel for help.

Tristan smiled happily at the sharks' handiwork.

Coach Fred turned to the others in the boat. "Looks like our job here is done."

"What about all the animals in the ship?" Sam asked.

"Don't worry," Ms. Sanchez answered. "We'll follow up on it. I'm sure they will be returned to the sea as soon as possible.

"Maybe we can help," Tristan suggested.

"We'll see," Coach said. "For now, let's get you back to the hotel, cleaned up, and rested. With a little luck, we'll have you all home in time for Christmas."

24

CHRISTMAS IN CAYMAN

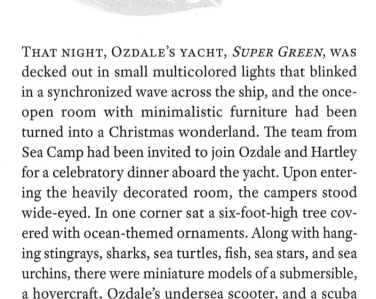

THAT NIGHT, OZDALE'S YACHT, *SUPER GREEN*, WAS decked out in small multicolored lights that blinked in a synchronized wave across the ship, and the once-open room with minimalistic furniture had been turned into a Christmas wonderland. The team from Sea Camp had been invited to join Ozdale and Hartley for a celebratory dinner aboard the yacht. Upon entering the heavily decorated room, the campers stood wide-eyed. In one corner sat a six-foot-high tree covered with ocean-themed ornaments. Along with hanging stingrays, sharks, sea turtles, fish, sea stars, and sea urchins, there were miniature models of a submersible, a hovercraft, Ozdale's undersea scooter, and a scuba diver. White rugs provided a snowy look, while bows of greenery spread throughout the room and hung on the walls made it seem like the group had just entered a forest. Hundreds of tiny white lights decorated the furniture and greenery. Christmas music played in the background, and a huge buffet had been laid out on the bar at the front of the room.

"Welcome, and job well done," Hartley said as they arrived. "You've done a great service for the island. And the stingrays, of course."

Ozdale stood nearby, grinning. He was leaning on a new silver cane wrapped in red ribbon like a candy cane. Another head popped out from under a table. Damien the Doberman seemed to be in agreement. Hugh jumped behind Tristan to avoid another potential slobber fest.

"It was our pleasure," Ms. Sanchez said.

Tristan almost blurted out that he wouldn't exactly call it a "pleasure." He, Sam, and Hugh were still having a hard time sitting down thanks to their emergency-chute landings. He was happy they saved the sea creatures and stopped the illegal collectors on the ship. But still, it was not what he'd call a pleasurable experience.

"Please, come in, relax, have something to eat," Ozdale encouraged.

The group wandered about the room, checking things out. Then they piled plates high with food and found seats.

"So what's going to happen to that cargo ship and crew?" Tristan asked, between mouthfuls of delicious roasted chicken and stuffing smothered in gravy.

"Did they find out where the animals were being taken?" Hugh added.

"Yeah, and, like, who was in that other boat?" Ryder wanted to know.

"Did they release all the animals?" Sam questioned.

Coach Fred held up his hands. "Whoa, there. One question at a time."

"I'm happy to report that the ship has been confiscated by the port authority here," Hartley told them. "It will never again be used to illegally collect or transport anything. The crew and captain are being detained on the island and questioned. So far, they've been unable to discover what the ship's true final destination was. There's some evidence it may have been headed to somewhere in the Middle East, possibly Dubai or Abu Dhabi."

"Dubai?" Tristan said.

"Actually, that's not all that surprising," Ms. Sanchez added. "Over the past several years, there's been a tremendous building boom there. Super luxury hotels and outrageous theme parks have been built—including an indoor ski slope in the desert. I wouldn't be surprised if someone over there is planning a mega over-the-top aquarium or marine park. And with their kind of money, developers can buy just about anything—legally or illegally. And as far as I know, in that part of the world there are no standards for the keeping of animals. Who knows what sort of deplorable conditions the marine life would have been kept in."

Hartley nodded. "The authorities are still working on it, and hopefully they'll discover who was behind the collecting and smuggling operation."

"What about the animals?" Sam asked again.

"Don't worry, we haven't forgotten about them. Tomorrow, a team will release the animals back into the sea. The folks at Oceanland have offered their assistance with the transportation and releases. As it turns out, one of their employees was secretly helping the smugglers on the side, using some of Oceanland's boats and equipment. The manager of the place feels terrible and wants to do anything he can to help."

"Can we help?" asked Sam hopefully.

All the teens turned to Coach Fred, waiting to see what he would say.

Ms. Sanchez nodded to Coach. At first he looked all serious, like it was a terrible idea. Then he broke out in a rare smile. "You got it. We'll stay one more night, help with the releases, and then head home. Right on, campers."

"And I'd like to offer my help as well," Ozdale announced. "Whatever I can do. Oh, and before I forget, I have a little something for each of you. I didn't have much time, but I hope you'll enjoy these small tokens of our gratitude for all that you've done. Merry Christmas!"

He nodded to Damien, who had just finished his own holiday meal in a bowl. The Doberman trotted to the bar and dragged out a big *Ozdale Industries* duffle bag.

"We each get our own rescue chute?" Tristan whispered to Hugh sarcastically.

"Now, let's see what we have here. Santa was very smart to leave it here for you," Ozdale laughed.

The others couldn't help but smile at the man's obvious enjoyment. One by one he pulled out gifts badly covered in silver-and-red wrapping paper. "Did the wrapping myself. Now, let's see, here's one for the lovely Ms. Sanchez." Ozdale handed her an almost neatly wrapped, small box. "Another for our fearless leader, Coach Fred." He passed him a less well-wrapped, soft package. "And of course, one each for Ryder, Rosina, Sam, Hugh, and Tristan."

The teens all gratefully accepted their gifts and said thanks. Then they sat awkwardly looking at the presents, not sure what the polite thing was to do next.

"Well, don't just sit there," Ozdale said, smiling expectantly. "Go ahead and open them!"

Ms. Sanchez unwrapped hers first. It was a pair of hanging silver earrings, each containing a small, striped, polished stone. "They're beautiful. Thank you, Mr. Ozdale."

"Oh, please. Call me Leo."

"The stone is Caymanite," Hartley told her. "Found only here in the Cayman Islands."

"Your turn, Coach," Ozdale said.

Coach Fred grimaced, like having fun and opening presents was utterly taxing to his patience. He precisely undid the tape and slowly began loosening the wrapping.

"Oh, for goodness' sake, tear it apart, man," Ozdale said. "You did see the wrapping job, right?"

That got the barest of smiles out of Coach before he tore open the silver-and-red paper. Inside was a black

T-shirt. He held it up and frowned. Written on the front was *Welcome to Hell*.

"You all didn't have a chance to visit the tourist site we talked about. But I thought I'd get you a little memento anyways. Seemed sort of appropriate."

"Yeah, Coach, you should wear that for Ocean Boot Camp," Tristan blurted out.

"What was that, Hunt?" Coach said, extremely seriously.

"Nothing, I mean . . ."

Then Coach Fred smiled. "Just kidding. I *love* it. Thank you."

The others turned to Sam as she unwrapped her gift. It was a blue minidress with white silhouettes of stingrays on it. "Cool. Thanks, Mr. Ozdale."

Ozdale stared at her.

"Leo, I mean."

"Rosina?" Ozdale said.

The teen sat staring oddly at the present, as if she was stunned at the thought of receiving a gift.

"Go ahead, open it," Tristan urged.

Rosina carefully undid the package. She too received a minidress with stingrays on it, only hers was in red. "Wow, thanks."

"Her—in a dress?" Ryder said. "I'd like to see that."

"Only if you're lucky," Rosina fired back.

The others laughed.

Ozdale then looked to Hugh. "Why don't you open yours next. After what happened, I thought you could use these."

Hugh looked puzzled as he undid the wrapping. Inside were swim trunks decorated with sharks. "Yeah, guess I could use a new pair since mine became the first-ever sea-star parachute."

"That was smart thinking, you three," Ozdale said to Tristan, Hugh, and Sam. "Maybe you'll be inventors like me someday."

Tristan and Ryder opened their gifts; they also received new shark shorts.

Ozdale then nodded to Hartley, who stood up and went to something large, about three feet tall by four feet wide. It was covered by a red cloth and leaning against the wall. "I thought there might be a nice place to hang this back at Sea Camp, again as a token of our appreciation for all that you've done." With a great flourish, he whipped off the red cloth.

"Awesome," Tristan said, staring at the painting that had been unveiled. Three gray stingrays with creamy-white underbellies seemed to soar across the canvas.

"Wicked," Sam added.

"Thank you both so much," Ms. Sanchez said. "We will proudly hang that up at Sea Camp and remember you with great fondness. Unfortunately, we don't have anything for you, but I'd like to extend an invitation to you both to come and visit us in Florida anytime."

"Oh, believe me, you've already given us more than we could ask for," Ozdale noted. "All those creatures alive and back home. It'll be a wonderful Christmas. Do you all have special plans?"

Tristan and the other teens explained what their

family typically did for the holiday. Everyone joined in the conversation except for Rosina. She sat quietly and stared at the floor.

"What about you, Rosina?" Ozdale asked. "Any special plans when you get home?"

She shook her head. Tristan noticed that again she appeared on the verge of tears. Ms. Sanchez went to the teen and sat beside her.

Tristan again wondered what was going on with Rosina. He suddenly realized he'd actually grown to like her and was kind of worried about her.

Rosina finally looked up and said to Ozdale, "For Christmas, I just want a job for my dad."

Everyone was silent.

Completely unfazed, Ozdale enthusiastically said, "Well, young lady, what does your father do?"

Rosina looked at the man. "He's a carpenter, builds things. Company he worked for went under, and now he says he's too old and no one will hire him."

"Too old? My bottom!" Ozdale told her. "Is he good at what he does?"

"Yeah, you should see all the cool things he's made."

"Well then, your father will come work for me. I can always use good workers, especially people that can build things!"

"Really?" Rosina said. "You're not joking again are you?"

"Of course not. It's a done deal. We'll work out the details later."

Rosina grinned and Tristan did a double take. He'd

never seen her smile like that before. It actually made her look—pretty.

"There's just one problem," Ozdale said.

Rosina's smile instantly faded.

"I forgot a present."

"For who?" Tristan asked, looking around.

Damien leapt up and twirled around like he was chasing his tail. The Doberman then sat beside Ozdale, his eyes wide with expectation. Ozdale reached into the now nearly empty duffle bag and pulled out a fuzzy, white, faceless teddy bear. Ozdale tossed the white toy. Damien leapt up to grab it. Tristan expected the dog to rip the thing apart, legs and arms to go flying, stuffing to pour out. Instead, Damien gently grasped the teddy bear, lay down, and nuzzled it.

Ozdale chuckled and affectionately pet the Doberman. They spent the next hour or so chatting about all that had happened since arriving in Grand Cayman, and discussing plans for tomorrow and the release of the rescued animals. It had been decided that the group from Sea Camp would go with the team heading to Stingray City. The other animals were being released into the waters around Cheeseburger Reef.

25

RETURN TO
STINGRAY CITY

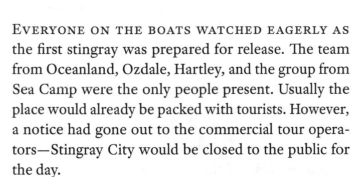

EVERYONE ON THE BOATS WATCHED EAGERLY AS the first stingray was prepared for release. The team from Oceanland, Ozdale, Hartley, and the group from Sea Camp were the only people present. Usually the place would already be packed with tourists. However, a notice had gone out to the commercial tour operators—Stingray City would be closed to the public for the day.

Anticipation grew as the stingray was tenderly raised from one of the tubs that had been ferried out to the sand bar. Tristan was helping to lift the ray. He tried to be as gentle as possible, his hands sinking into the ray's soft, white underbelly. The animal was very heavy. Silently, Tristan repeatedly tried to calm the ray and explain what was happening.

Are we there yet? Tristan heard the ray ask. It was about the twentieth time the ray had asked the question.

Almost, Tristan thought. *Just a few steps to the side of the boat.*

Ooo, that tickles, the ray told him.

Tristan chuckled. The two women from Oceanland helping to carry the ray looked at Tristan funnily. He ignored them and focused on moving carefully toward a gap in the rail of the pontoon boat. Ozdale stood nearby, watching.

"Wonder what it's thinking?" Ozdale said, winking at Tristan.

A woman from Oceanland shrugged unknowingly.

Tristan smiled. *Okay, get ready,* he said silently to the ray.

I'm way past ready, bobo, the ray replied.

It was slowgoing carrying the large, thickset stingray. The animal was at least four feet wide. The local operators had fondly named her Big Bertha. Tristan decided it might be best not to tell the ray that. He knew sea creatures could be quite sensitive. As they neared the side of the boat, Tristan's foot slid on the wet deck. He nearly did a split and would have dumped the big stingray if Ozdale hadn't reached out and grabbed Tristan's arm to help him.

"Thanks," Tristan said sheepishly to Ozdale. He then apologized to the ray for almost dropping her.

"Okay, careful now," the woman from Oceanland instructed. "Lower her slowly and then we'll slide her into the water."

Tristan bent down, lowering his side of the heavy stingray. It was an awkward movement. He felt the ray slipping from his fingers, or maybe it was attempting to jump. He couldn't be sure. The ray slid out of their hands and dove headfirst smoothly into the water.

Be free! Tristan thought.

Once in the ocean, the stingray immediately flicked its wide, powerful wing-like fins. It soared gracefully through the water. The ray made a quick U-turn and doubled back to the boat. The stingray slapped its fins on the surface, splashing the people leaning over to watch. Tristan knew it was happy and thanking them. He went to the next tub to help release another of the captured rays. Sam, Hugh, Rosina, and Ryder were on other boats. They all began helping to release more of the returning animals.

Stingrays from all around had come to welcome back the kidnapped rays. It was a joyous in-water reunion—a stingray party. Some rays swam swiftly through the growing mob, brushing against the newly released rays. Other stingrays did tight little circles around the returning rays. At least one hundred sting-rays were now swarming about the boats.

By just after noon, all the stingrays had been re-leased. They were mingling with their relatives and friends. A smorgasbord of chopped-up fish and squid had been tossed into the water for the rays. It had been decided that no one would go in the water that day. They wanted to let the stingrays reunite, feed, and re-acclimate without humans getting in the way. Soon the boats began to depart.

Before leaving, Tristan lay down on his stomach on the boat's deck. He put his hand in the water to pet some passing stingrays and listened. They were saying things like *'Thanks, bobo,' 'Come back soon,'* and *'Want some squid?'* Tristan didn't even mind hearing a ton of voices in his head all at the same time.

26

STINKY SAVES THE DAY

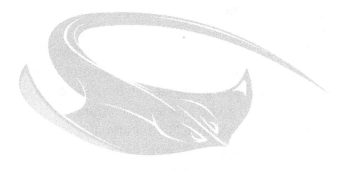

THE TEENS HAD ONLY A FEW HOURS LEFT IN GRAND Cayman. They were scheduled to fly out that night.

In the boys' room, Tristan, Hugh, and Ryder were packing their bags.

"So, what do you guys wanna do until we leave?" Ryder asked.

"Coach said to rest and pack," Hugh answered.

"Rest? Who wants to rest?" Ryder said. "Besides, check out the water." He pointed out the sliding back door of their room. The sun sparkled off the exceptionally calm, bright-blue ocean. "Couldn't get a much nicer day than this. Let's go for a swim!"

"I don't know," Hugh said, looking to Tristan.

Tristan was tired but also still wound up from the joy and excitement of releasing the stingrays. The ocean did look very inviting. It almost felt like it was calling him—*come in, Tristan. Jump in.* "Hey, remember what Sophie said? There's a mermaid statue out on the reef behind the hotel."

"Yeah," Hugh responded.

"Would be pretty cool to see it."

"Like, I totally wanna see it," Ryder said. "Let's go!"

Hugh looked at the other two boys. "But what if someone sees us?"

"So what?" Tristan said. "We haven't taken the pills in a while; I doubt any webbing will come out now. We'll be like regular kids going for a swim. Besides, no one said we couldn't go for a swim or anything."

"C'mon, Hugh. Let's do it," Ryder urged.

"Okay, okay. Let's see if the girls want to come."

After grabbing some towels and tiptoeing out of their room, Tristan quietly knocked on the door to the girls' room.

Rosina came to the door. Upon seeing Tristan, she smoothed her hair and straightened her clothes. "Hey, Tristan, what's up?"

Sam was looking on from behind Rosina and rolled her eyes.

"We're gonna go for a swim to see the mermaid statue. You guys wanna come?"

Rosina smiled shyly. "Are *you* going?"

Tristan looked at her, confused. "Didn't I just say that?" He looked past Rosina. "Sam?"

"Sure."

The teens made their way along an asphalt walkway behind the hotel. Coach Fred and Ms. Sanchez were nowhere to be seen. They came to a big, square cut in the rocks along the shore. It was a shallow pool connected to the ocean. Tristan gazed through the wonderfully clear water in the sea pool, searching for creatures. There was only white sand.

"This is so cool," Sam noted.

"Like, excellent," Ryder added.

They placed their towels and T-shirts on a short concrete wall nearby. Ryder then pulled something out of his pocket and looked around to see if anyone was watching. "Hey, check it out. I snagged these from Coach's bag-o-pills a while ago." He was holding out a handful of red algae pills. "Just in case we might, you know, need them sometime."

"You *did not*," Sam said.

"Yup," Ryder said, smirking. "Do you really want to swim all the way out to find the mermaid without webbing?"

No one answered. Tristan knew that if people were around, they shouldn't take the pills, but he really wanted to. It was so much more fun swimming with webbed hands and feet. Without them, he'd be so slow and couldn't stay down very long. They'd be like normal people. Tristan glanced around. He didn't see any swimmers or divers nearby, and nobody seemed to be watching from shore.

Ryder gulped down a pill and held out the rest to the others. Rosina stared at Tristan, clearly waiting to see what he would do.

"We'll stay away from anyone who's around," Sam said. "Right?"

"Right," Ryder said, confidently.

The temptation was overpowering. *Besides,* Tristan thought, *if someone comes along, we can just hide our webbing.* Feeling confident, he grabbed a pill. Before he could think any more about it, he swallowed it. Sam did the same and then so did Rosina. Hugh looked on, shaking his head. But after a few minutes, he gave in and took a pill too.

Ryder and Tristan jumped excitedly into the pool. Sam did a cannonball. Hugh and Rosina took the nearby stairs. By the time the teens were out in the ocean, their webbing had appeared. The water was clear, cool, and refreshing. Tristan happily kicked his feet and dove. He skimmed along the smooth light-tan rock bottom. There were grooves and pockets filled with sand. Scattered about were small yellowy-green coral heads and purple sea fans. He saw a multicolored parrotfish and then a pair of yellow butterflyfish. Tristan rose to the surface for air and looked for the others. The group was treading water nearby.

"Which way?" Hugh asked.

"I think it's farther offshore," Sam answered.

The teens dove and headed seaward into deeper water. Suddenly, a flash of silver raced by. Seconds later, a four-foot-long barracuda hung in the water about a foot away from Tristan. The teens all stopped and stared at the fish. It stared back. The fish's mouth hung partially open, putting its long stiletto teeth on display. The campers swam on, and the fish stayed right beside them. Tristan went to the surface and the others followed.

STINKY SAVES THE DAY

Tristan turned to Hugh. "What's up with the barracuda? It's kinda freaking me out."

Hugh laughed, which was not the reaction Tristan
expected, especially from Hugh.

"Remember, barracuda are territorial," Hugh told
them. "This is where it lives. It's just curious about us."

"Can you tell it to be curious a little farther away?"
Tristan muttered. "Hey, does it know where the mermaid statue is?"

Hugh swam to the barracuda and submerged. He
popped up a minute later. "Said it would be happy to
show us."

"Can you also ask it to let us know if it sees any
scuba divers or other people around?" Sam suggested,
holding up her webbed hands.

"Good idea," Hugh replied, before ducking back
underwater.

The teens dove down, following the barracuda. The
water was now about twenty feet deep. Big patches and
mounds of bumpy brown coral littered the bottom. As
they swam farther offshore, the patches of coral co-
alesced into a rolling reef. Between the knobby coral
hills were deep grooves filled with sand that stretched
seaward into deeper water. Fish swam in and around
the reef. Tristan recognized two large French angelfish.
They were flat, black-and-yellow, triangular-shaped
fish. The duo swam side by side, as if exploring the underwater world in tandem. Schools of small bright-blue
fish hovered over the coral. A small sea turtle swam by.

Following the barracuda, they swam on. Tristan

suddenly remembered to look around for any divers in the area. There were no bubbles or signs of anyone scuba diving or snorkeling. Tristan headed up for air. The water had deepened to about fifty feet. The teens again gathered on the surface.

"The barracuda hasn't seen any divers since this morning," Hugh told them. "And the mermaid statue is just over that mound of coral there." He pointed underwater to their right.

"Still, keep an eye out," Sam said. "If someone sees our webs out here and Coach finds out, we're doomed."

Totally, thought Tristan.

The group dove down and headed to the big mound of brown star coral to their right. Like a school of giant fish, they swam together over and around the coral. Then Tristan saw it. He kicked hard to be the first one to reach the statue. Once there, he sidled up next to the mermaid, put his arm around her shoulders, and waved. Tristan then studied the undersea statue. The mermaid was greenish tan and a little blotchy looking. She stood erect on a base in the sand with her back arched. One hand was down and a little bit out from her side, while the other was held up as if she was about to wave. The statue's wavy hair streamed back from her face. Tristan thought her expression seemed kind of serious, like she was deep in thought or something.

The teens then took turns posing with the mermaid. Hugh pretended to shake her hand. Sam curtsied and then posed cheek to cheek. Rosina stood beside the mermaid and tried to emulate her pose. That made the others laugh so hard they had to go to the surface for air. Ryder dove back down and the others followed. He swam to the front of the statue, put his lips against the mermaid's mouth, and pretended to make out with her. Bubbles of laughter erupted around Tristan and the other teens, sending them back to the surface.

Tristan was completely caught up in their mermaid fun. He forgot about everything else, including being on the lookout for divers. That all changed when he heard a strange deep hum in the water. He saw Sam stop abruptly and look around. She'd heard it too. They both twisted around, searching for what was making the noise. It didn't sound like a boat engine. Tristan noticed movement to their left. Turning toward it, he saw something big and dark in the distance. It took him a moment to realize what it was and that it was headed their way. *Oh, no,* Tristan thought. They were about to be in big trouble, very deep doo-doo. It was the local tourist submarine.

Tristan shook his head, disgusted with himself. He had completely forgotten the other thing Sophie had told them—the submarine came by every afternoon to view the mermaid. He and Sam tried to get the others' attention. But they were still busy horsing around at the statue. By the time they got the others to notice the sub, it was so close Tristan could see the long row of round viewports along one side. He looked around frantically for a place to hide. The submarine came closer. Tristan could now make out faces plastered up against the viewports. If they swam for it, surely the people in the submarine would notice them and their webbed feet. Tristan squeezed his fingers and toes tight together to hide his webbing, showing the others what he was doing. They did it too. But then Tristan realized that five thirteen-year-olds hovering fifty feet down without scuba gear would be unusual—to say the least. The campers were about to be put on show, the main attraction—an underwater spectacle. Suddenly, a gray blur raced past the teens and whooshed by the submarine.

The sub instantly stopped moving. A large dolphin circled the sub once and then stopped on the side opposite the teens. The faces Tristan had seen before disappeared as the people inside scrambled to the viewports on the sub's other side. The dolphin hovered in front of them. It then swam slowly closer as if looking in. At one point the dolphin rose up briefly and glanced over at Tristan and the other teens. Tristan could swear the creature flicked its head, indicating they should swim away now. He turned to Sam. She nodded and motioned for the others to follow as she took off toward the coral mound behind the mermaid statue.

The dolphin made several more slow passes in front of the tourists. It did corkscrew rolls and pretended to rush the windows in a fun, teasing sort of way. Meanwhile, the campers swam as fast as they could away from the mermaid statue and the sub. They swam around coral mounds and up a sandy groove toward shore. When they were past the reef and back in about fifteen feet of water, they popped up to the surface, gasping for air.

A few minutes later, the dolphin raced by, and a

wave of water sent the group tumbling. The dolphin circled back and swam toward the teens. It stopped abruptly and hovered in front of Sam. Then it nipped at her toes.

"What the heck is with that dolphin?" Hugh said.

"It just saved us from being seen is what," Sam answered, playfully pushing the dolphin away from her feet.

"Yeah, but what's it doing now?" Tristan asked, right before the dolphin turned and headbutted him in the chest. He went rolling backward again.

Sam started to laugh, and the other teens stared at her like she was ready for the loony bin.

"It's Stinky," Sam said.

"Yeah, that wacko dolphin from South Sound," Hugh added.

Tristan swam back, spitting out seawater. "Hey, why me? What did I do?"

"No," Sam told them. "He thinks he's being funny, playing."

"Funny?" Tristan asked.

The dolphin swam toward them, and all but Sam backed away. This time, Stinky slowed and stopped beside Sam. She reached out and caressed his smooth gray skin. The dolphin lightly butted her with his beak. "See, it's fine. Stinky just didn't realize that what he was doing was scaring us."

"Yeah, well, tell him getting creamed in the chest is definitely not fun or funny," Tristan said.

"He's just playing," Sam repeated. "If you were another dolphin, what he did would seem like fun."

"If you say so," Tristan said. "But if Stinky hadn't diverted the attention of those people on the sub, they would have seen us for sure. Thank him for us." He rubbed his chest. "And tell him to play a little softer next time."

Sam rubbed the dolphin some more and thanked him for them.

"So how come Stinky is all by himself?" Hugh asked. "Don't dolphins usually live in pods?"

Sam ducked underwater to talk to the dolphin. After a minute or two, she came up. "Stinky got lost from his pod in a storm. Every time he finds a new pod and tries to join, they chase him away. That's why he's always looking for someone to play with. I think he's sad. Stinky feels like he's all alone and doesn't have a home."

"I know how he feels," Rosina mumbled.

"What?" Hugh asked her.

"Oh, nothing," Rosina said, shaking her head like she wished she hadn't said anything.

"Is it because your dad lost his job?" Tristan asked, thinking about what she had said on Ozdale's yacht. "You're not alone. You've got us. And you have a home, right?"

"Where *do* you live?" Hugh asked. "You've never said."

Rosina turned away so the others wouldn't see her face. "Never mind. I shouldn't have said anything."

The dolphin left Sam's side and sidled up next to Rosina, pushing her surprisingly gently with his beak.

"C'mon, Rosina," Tristan said encouragingly. "What are you talking about?"

Rosina took a deep breath before speaking. "Look, like I said, my dad lost his job a couple of years ago, and Mom, well, she hasn't been around for a while. When Dad couldn't find another job, we . . . we got kicked out of our house. Couldn't make the payments."

"Where are you living now?" Sam asked.

Rosina shook her head and stroked the dolphin as her eyes welled up. "I didn't want you guys to find out. We're living in shelters, and sometimes in a cheap hotel, if dad can get some work."

Tristan had heard about kids and families living on the street, but he'd never met any. It all made sense now. Why Rosina had acted so mean and was kind of a mess when they first arrived at camp. Why, for so long, she was distant and snarly with them. Tristan realized he shouldn't be so quick to judge people. You never knew what was going on in their lives. It also made him more appreciative of his family and home, even his super-overprotective mother and annoying sister.

Ryder swam to Rosina and put his hand on her shoulder. "Yeah, but Leo is going to give your dad a job. Then you can get a house."

"Yeah," the rest of them said.

Rosina pushed Ryder away and looked at him like she had no idea who he was. "What happened to you, surfer boy? Someone put nice in that pill you took?"

Tristan smiled. *That* was the Rosina they knew and now liked.

They headed back to shore. For the entire way, Stinky swam with them. At the sea pool, they said good-bye to the dolphin. Rosina seemed particularly sorry to see him go.

The group climbed out of the water and dried off. Then they waited until their webbing was all but gone before heading back to their rooms. On the way, they passed the thatched-roof beach bar. Someone yelled, "Hey, campers!"

It was Ms. Sanchez. She was sitting at the bar beside Ozdale. They were drinking fancy fruit drinks with umbrellas in the glasses.

The teens froze, hoping they weren't about to get in trouble. They all waved super awkwardly. Ms. Sanchez waved back distractedly and turned to Ozdale. The campers ran for their rooms.

Sam whispered to Tristan, "I think Ms. Sanchez likes Mr. Ozdale."

"Yeah," Tristan said, raising his eyebrows with a smirk.

"I think its sweet," Rosina added.

"Like, yuck!" Ryder groaned.

Once inside their room, Hugh fell onto one of the beds. "I think I'm ready for a little less excitement."

"Yeah, some boring time at home sounds kinda good," Tristan agreed.

27

GOING HOME

THE SEA CAMP JET TOOK OFF FROM GRAND CAY-
man, and soon everyone but the pilot was napping. A
little more than an hour later, they landed in Miami.
The atmosphere in the airport was more cheery than
usual, being that it was Christmas Eve. Before each
of the teens was put on a flight home, they said their
good-byes.

Rosina hugged Sam. "Merry Christmas, Sam."

"Merry Christmas, Rosina."

Tristan watched the two girls. He was glad they
seemed to be getting along better, or at least not glaring daggers at one another. He never really understood
why girls acted so weird sometimes.

Rosina then approached Tristan. "Thanks for being
so nice about my dad and all."

"No problem. Must be tough."

"Yeah, but now that you guys know and everyone's been cool about it, I feel better."

Tristan nodded. "And I'm sure Leo will give your dad a job like he said."

Rosina smiled and gave Tristan a hug. "Have a good Christmas, Tristan." She then handed him a slip of paper. "Here's my phone number. Call me."

Tristan didn't know what to say. "Uh, yeah. Okay."

"Bye," Rosina said, waving as she walked away.

Sam came over and stared at the paper with the girl's number on it.

"What?" Tristan said.

"She likes you," Sam told him.

"Yeah, she likes you too."

"Not that way."

"Your head's full of seawater, Sam. We're barely friends."

"Uh-huh," Sam said. "Anyway, Merry Christmas, Tristan. I guess I'll see you at camp next summer."

"Yeah," Tristan answered. "Maybe we'll get to ride a shark again together." He wanted to say more to Sam, like how he liked holding her hand in the cargo ship and that he would miss her. But he couldn't seem to find the right words. So instead he just stood there, once again all tongue-tied.

Sam seemed unsure of what to say, too. "Okay, well, stay in touch."

"Okay. Uh, you too."

Sam stepped toward him. Tristan hesitated, even

pulling back a bit. They hugged, sort of—more like a hurried, joint pat on the back. Sam then waved and turned to say good-bye to Ms. Sanchez. Hugh hit Tristan on the arm. "Smooth move, there, *bobo*."

"What?" Tristan asked, though he knew exactly what Hugh meant.

Hugh just shook his head. "Good luck at home. Before you know it, we'll be back at camp for the summer."

"Have you figured out what you're going to tell your mom about Grand Cayman?"

"I think I'll just tell her the parts that won't freak her out. Otherwise I'll never go on another mission."

"Yeah," Tristan said. "Me too. I'm not going to lie, just leave out the scary parts."

"I wonder who was behind the whole thing?"

"What do you mean?" Tristan asked.

"You know," Hugh said. "Who was paying for the cargo ship and their operation? Where were those animals headed?"

"Sounds like we may never know," Tristan noted.

Just then, Coach Fred joined the two boys. "Okay, everyone else has their tickets home. Hunt, Haverford, here are yours." He handed them airplane tickets. "We'll walk you to security where each of you will be met by an airline representative to get you to your flight. Do what they say, and no funny business."

"No problem, Coach," Tristan said, thinking that after getting sucked aboard a cargo ship full of criminals and escaping via the rescue chute, making their way to an airplane was no big deal. Definitely something they could do on their own.

The teens all said their final good-byes and waved as each was led to their flight home.

28

THE GREEN SLIME

CHRISTMAS AND NEW YEAR'S EVE CAME AND went, and the months passed by. Tristan was back into the routine of going to school and pretending to be a normal kid. The excitement of his Grand Cayman adventure faded. There was no talking to or riding on sharks, no webbed hands and feet, and no saving sea creatures, or even talking about it. He texted Sam and Hugh off and on and heard that Rosina and her father had moved to Washington, DC, where Ozdale Industries' headquarters was located. Tristan was still curious about who had been behind the smuggling operation on the *Dawn Oasis* and regularly searched the Internet looking for answers.

One Sunday, Tristan was in his room, once again perusing the Internet for news or information related to the events in Grand Cayman. When he opened CNN's Web site, he was immediately drawn to one of the headlines: "Commercial Real Estate Mogul J.P. Rickerton Indicted." The article went on to say he'd been charged with wire fraud, money laundering, and illegal trade in historical artifacts. Rickerton had been captured in Monte Carlo, Monaco, was being held in isolation, and awaited extradition to the United States. Tristan was especially gratified to read that the authorities expected a long prison sentence once the man was convicted. He let out a giant sigh of relief, thinking, *That's at least one more criminal nutjob taken care of.*

After he finished reading the article, Tristan clicked back to the main Web site to peruse the other news. Another headline grabbed his attention: "Green Slime Cancels America's Cup Sailing Race." Tristan clicked on the story and read:

> *An unusually dense bloom of green algae has filled the harbor in Newport, Rhode Island. Dead fish litter the surface and all boat traffic has come to a halt. The America's Cup race was set to begin this week, but due to the algal bloom, it has been postponed. The smell of decomposing fish and algae has driven tourists away, and even the local residents are fleeing the area. Experts have been called in to determine the cause, and city employees are working around the clock to clean up the mess.*
>
> *Across the globe, numerous cities have reported similar algal blooms and fish kills. Manatees and dolphins along Florida's west coast are showing*

signs of a potentially related illness. Scientists are looking for a cause and possible connections. More to come as the story develops.

Tristan sat staring at the computer screen. He was about to text Hugh and Sam about the news when there was a knock on his bedroom door.

"Tristan," his father called out. "Director Davis just called. Seems there's an international emergency and he's calling in all the Sea Campers."

Tristan opened the door and smiled at his father. "When do I leave?"

NOTE FROM
THE AUTHOR

THE STORY HERE IS FICTION, BUT MUCH OF THE adventure is based on reality. Stingray City in Grand Cayman is a true wonder to behold. I was lucky enough to get a private introduction from longtime ocean advocate, celebrity wildlife painter, scientist, and local resident, Guy Harvey. Some of you may have recognized him as the character of Guy Hartley in the book! Guy took me to Stingray City on his boat in the early morning, before the regular tour operators arrived. We jumped in the water and were immediately swarmed, surrounded, and mauled by stingrays. It was fantastic! I loved it. Guy brought along a bucket full of cut-up lionfish. We proceeded to feed the rays by hand, and one did the twirling pizza-dough routine on my hand. The Guy Harvey Research Institute is working with local leaders, along with veterinarians and scientists, to study the rays at Stingray City and monitor the impact of visitors and feeding. As part of their work, they regularly tag the stingrays. In 2012, some stingrays really did go missing from Stingray City. Four of the rays, which had been tagged, were later discovered at a local dolphin park. Stingrays and sharks are now fully protected in Cayman waters, and strict regulations have been put in place to reduce the handling of rays at Stingray City. Research has shown that although their natural behavior has been altered by hand-feeding at Stingray City, the stingrays are very healthy. In fact, a large percentage of the females during one survey were found to be pregnant.

On a boat ride back from a trip to the deeper dive site at Stingray City, a lone dolphin followed us. It was a resident dolphin known for harassing divers and causing trouble—Stinky is real. Though I hear he hasn't been seen for a while.

Another aspect of the story that is real is Sunset House. It is a small, cozy hotel in Grand Cayman that caters especially to divers, and has a fantastic view and restaurant. And yes, there really is a mermaid statue on the reef, just a short swim away from the dock. A tourist submarine regularly makes visits to the mermaid, and it is a favorite dive site for visitors. I had a terrific time scuba diving with the guides at Sunset House. One of my favorite sites was Cheeseburger Reef, also known as Fish Pot Reef. Mini mountains of coral rise up from the sand, large tarpon swim about, and there are several twisting tunnels, or "swim-throughs," in the reef.

Grand Cayman also hosts the world's only blue iguanas. Conservation efforts have brought them back from the brink of extinction, and they are quite the sight. I'll post some photos at www.tristan-hunt.com. And of course, if you are in Grand Cayman, plan to make a stop and mail a postcard from Hell.

Tiger sharks are known to cruise Cayman waters. Researchers studying tiger sharks have discovered they are indeed curious creatures, have exceptionally strong teeth, and will eat just about anything. Within their stomachs, scientists have found other sharks, birds, boots, tires, and, yes, even a bag of potatoes. Adult tiger sharks also eat sea turtles. They are ambush predators and have distinctive black stripes on their backs.

The beginning of the book takes place in Monterey, California, at the wonderful and world-renowned Monterey Bay Aquarium. I was fortunate to visit when jellyfish from around the world were being featured. All of the species mentioned in the book are real. Of course, I had a little fictional fun with what the animals at the aquarium might be thinking and some of their personal problems. If you're visiting Monterey, the aquarium is not to be missed, and please say hello to the sea otters and giant Pacific octopus for me. Diving or kayaking in the kelp beds is also highly recommended. And with care, you don't really have to worry about getting tangled up in the kelp. Did you know that kelp is the fastest-growing seaweed on the planet? In one day, bull kelp can grow almost a foot. In one year, giant kelp can get to be one-hundred feet long! Kelp forests along the California coast are shadowy worlds rich with marine life. The seaweed creates a canopy and habitat that provides protection from predators, a relative calm in waves and currents, and an extensive menu for ocean diners. Along with the hungry and playful sea otters, hundreds of other species make their home in California's forests of kelp.

And remember in the story how the music from the movie *Jaws* was piped into the giant kelp tank while the teens were cleaning the viewing window? My fellow divers once played the same practical joke on me at night while I was working. They put a hydrophone in the water, and I really did hear that music. It was kinda creepy!

One last note here. Illegal fishing and collecting are enormous problems worldwide. In the United States, there are strict rules governing fisheries and collecting. Unfortunately, such rules do not uniformly exist throughout the world. For instance, it is illegal to touch, harass, and collect marine mammals in US waters. That is not true everywhere. And even where good policies are in place, they are often extremely hard to enforce. I am strongly opposed to the killing or capture of wild whales and dolphins. I do, however, support rescue and rehabilitation efforts. If such animals cannot be released into the wild, they should be kept in sufficient spaces, well fed, and treated with the utmost care and respect.

Most people will never see a sea otter in the wild or watch a leopard shark swim lazily by in the sea. Aquariums provide a critical view into the ocean world—one that opens people's hearts to caring and conservation.

To learn more about the science in *Stingray City* and the author, to contact me, and to see photos of the animals and habitats described, please visit www.tristan-hunt.com. And send me a note or tweet (@elprager), or look me up on Facebook. I love to hear from readers. And as always, dive in!

ACKNOWLEDGEMENTS

My sincere thanks to everyone who helped make *Stingray City* possible. To my friends and family, who are always at the ready to provide passionate encouragement and support. To Keith and Karin Sahm at Sunset House for their support and generosity. I truly consider you both great friends, and look forward to having more fun with you in Grand Cayman soon. Thanks also to the Sunset House dive guides for their excellent assistance and diving. And of course, a big thanks to Guy Harvey for my fantastic introduction to Stingray City, and for all that he does to preserve and protect the ocean and its wonderful diversity of life. Appreciation also goes to Hank Armstrong and everyone else at the Monterey Bay Aquarium for a fantastic behind-the-scenes tour and all the work you do to educate the public about the ocean, marine organisms, and conservation. And to Carl Safina and all the folks at the Safina Center for making me a fellow and giving me the opportunity to work with such a great group of like-minded people.

The Tristan Hunt and the Sea Guardians series and this book would not be possible without the efforts of Janell Agyeman and everyone at Mighty Media Press, including Nancy Tuminelly, Sara Lien Edelman, Sammy Bosch, Carolyn Bernhardt, Chris Long, Emily O'Malley, and Anders Hanson. Special thanks to managing editor, Lauren Kukla, along with Rebecca Felix and Karen Kenney for their excellent editing and improvement of the text. And of course to Antonio Javier Caparo, whose drawings for the cover and maps I wait to see with bated breath.

And to all the fans who have written such wonderful reviews, tweeted, e-mailed, or contacted me through Facebook, you are truly what inspire me.

ABOUT THE AUTHOR

WITH HER ABILITY TO MAKE SCIENCE FUN AND understandable for people of all ages, Dr. Ellen Prager, a marine scientist and author in Florida, has built a national reputation as a spokesperson on earth and ocean science issues. She has appeared on *The Today Show*, *Good Morning America*, CNN, CBS, NPR, The Discovery Channel, and more. Dr. Prager has participated in research expeditions to locations including the Galapagos Islands, Papua New Guinea, Fiji, and throughout the Caribbean. Formerly the chief scientist at the world's only undersea research station in the Florida Keys, she now acts as the science advisor to the Celebrity Cruise ship *Xpedition* in the Galapagos. Dr. Prager lives in St. Petersburg, Florida, where she spends her days writing, consulting, and spending as much time on and in the ocean as possible.

Dive into teamtristan.com to find an exclusive, full-color graphic novel excerpt of *The Shark Whisperer*

"... an underwater Harry Potter ..."

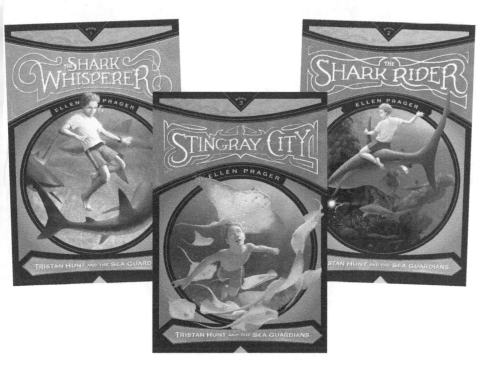

TRISTAN HUNT AND THE SEA GUARDIANS

Tristan Hunt can talk to sharks!

And his friends have even stranger skills. When Tristan is invited to attend an ocean-themed summer camp, he learns how to use his talents in ways he never dreamed. Join Tristan and the Sea Guardians on daring adventures as they fight evil and solve mysteries to protect the ocean and its animals.

Available at Amazon, Barnes and Noble, or your favorite indie bookstore.